VIRGINIA WOOLF

Mrs
Dalloway

戴洛維夫人

Adaptation and activities by Richard Larkham
Illustrated by Antonio Marinoni

U0063684

The Commercial Press

Contents 目錄

故事錄音開始和結束的標記
start ▶ **stop** ■

MAIN CHARACTERS

Clarissa Dalloway

Peter Walsh

Richard Dalloway

Sally Seton

Lucrezia Warren Smith

Septimus Warren Smith

Elizabeth Dalloway

Miss Kilman

Hugh Whitbread

Sir William Bradshaw

Dr Holmes

Lady Bradshaw

Aunt Helena

Ellie Henderson

Vocabulary

1 Read the blurb on the back of this book. *Mrs Dalloway* is about what happens to a small group of people on the day of a London party in the early 1920s. What words would you expect to find in the story? Use this word map to write down your ideas.

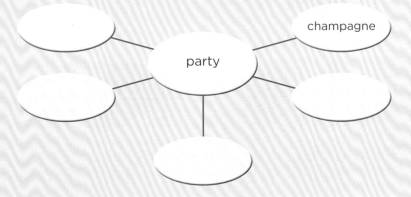

2 In Chapter One, we are introduced to the main character of this book, Clarissa Dalloway. Look at the front cover and make a list to describe her.

Mrs Dalloway seems:

_____

_____

_____

_____

_____

Writing

3 This chapter is called *An Eventful Visit to the Florist's*.
Can you imagine what happens when Clarissa goes out to buy
flowers? Write your prediction here... and then read to find out
what actually happened!

_____

_____

_____

4 The story of *Mrs Dalloway* in set in London. Write a list of the
streets and places you know of this city.

_____

_____

_____

Reading Comprehension

5 At one point Clarissa says that she *'always had the feeling that
it was very, very dangerous to live even one day'*. What do you
think she means? Do you agree with her?

_____

_____

_____

Speaking

6 Think about the title of this book. Why, for example, isn't it
called *Mrs Dalloway's Party* or *An Important Occasion*? What
does Virginia Woolf want to say with this title?

Chapter One

An Eventful Visit to the Florist's

▶ 2   Mrs Dalloway said she would buy the flowers herself.

Lucy had enough work to do; Rumpelmayer's workmen were coming to take the doors off. And what a fresh morning it was, thought Clarissa Dalloway… just like being at the seaside.

On days like this at Bourton, as a girl of eighteen, she had burst open the French windows[1] and plunged[2] into the fresh, calm open air. Yet she also remembered standing at the open window, serious, thinking that something terrible was about to happen. She would stand and look at the flowers and the trees and the birds — until Peter Walsh said, perhaps at breakfast, 'Talking to the vegetables, were you?' Peter Walsh — he would be coming back from India soon; Clarissa remembered his eyes, his pocket-knife, his smile and his grumpiness[3].

Clarissa waited on the kerb[4] for a van to pass. Meanwhile, Scrope Purvis saw her and thought (as much as he knew his next-door neighbour in Westminster): a charming woman, full of energy, even though she is over fifty and has gone[5] very white since her illness.

Clarissa recalled that she had lived in Westminster for over twenty years now. As she crossed Victoria Street, Big Ben struck; first of all the musical warning, then the hour. Boom! She wondered why most people in this city loved life so much, amidst[6] the traffic; and this was

1. **the French windows:** 通往花園的落地窗
2. **plunged:** 跳進
3. **grumpiness:** 壞脾氣
4. **kerb:** 行人路邊
5. **has gone:** 這裏指頭髮變得
6. **amidst:** 在……之間

what *she* loved: life; London; this moment in mid-June.

The War[1] was over, thank Heaven. The King and Queen were at Buckingham Palace. And everywhere, there was activity in this grey-blue early morning air; and Clarissa, too, loved it because she was going to give her party that night. How strange, then, walking into St James's Park, was the silence, the ducks swimming slowly — and who was that walking along? Her old dear, admirable friend Hugh Whitbread!

'Good-morning to you, Clarissa!' said Hugh, rather extravagantly[2], 'Where are you off to?'

'I love walking in London,' said Mrs Dalloway. 'Really it's better than walking in the country.'

Other people came to London to see exhibitions — the Whitbreads came to London 'to see doctors'. Clarissa had visited Evelyn Whitbread many times in a nursing home[3]. Was Evelyn ill again? Nothing serious, said Hugh. And as he quickly moved away, assuring her that he and Evelyn would be at her party, Clarissa felt aware of her hat. Not the right hat for the early morning, was that it? Hugh always made her feel a little underdressed — but he *was* a good person, though he nearly drove Richard mad, and Peter Walsh had never forgiven her for liking Hugh.

How she and Peter had argued! He said she would marry a Prime Minister and stand at the top of a staircase; the perfect hostess, he called her (she had cried about that in her bedroom), she had the makings of[4] the perfect hostess, he said.

She had been right not to marry Peter Walsh. For in marriage there must be a little independence between people living together

1. **The War:** 第一次世界大戰
2. **extravagantly:** 浮誇地
3. **nursing home:** 護老院
4. **had the makings of:** 具備足夠資格

day in day out[1] in the same house; which Richard gave her, and she him. (Where was he this morning for instance?) But with Peter everything had to be shared; and when, in the little garden at Bourton by the fountain, she had to break with him[2] or they would have been destroyed, she was convinced; though there was sadness in her heart for years; and then the shocking moment when someone told her at a concert that he had married a woman he met on the boat going to India! He was quite happy, he assured her — although he had never done a thing that they had talked of; his whole life had been a failure. It made Clarissa angry still.

She had reached the Park gates. She stood for a moment, looking at the omnibuses[3] in Piccadilly.

She felt very young; at the same time unspeakably old. She had a perpetual[4] sense of being out, out, far out to sea and alone; she always had the feeling that it was very, very dangerous to live even one day. She knew nothing; no language, no history; she hardly ever read a book now; but to her all this was absolutely absorbing.

Her only gift was knowing people almost by instinct. Did it matter then, she asked herself, that she must inevitably cease[5] to exist completely; all this must go on without her; that somehow in the streets of London, she survived, Peter survived, lived in each other, she being part of the trees at home; of the house there; part of people she had never met.

But what was she dreaming as she looked into Hatchards' shop window?

She read in the book spread open:

---

1. day in day out: 每一天
2. break with him: 和他分手
3. omnibuses: 公共馬車
4. perpetual: 永久的
5. cease: 停止

Fear no more the heat o' the sun
Nor the furious winter's rages[1].

There were a lot of books, but none that seemed exactly right to take to Evelyn Whitbread in her nursing home; nothing that would amuse her.

Clarissa turned and walked back towards Bond Street, annoyed, because it was silly to have other reasons for doing things. She would have preferred to be like Richard, who did things for themselves, but half the time she did things to make people think this or that.

Bond Street early in the morning fascinated her; its shops. She paused for a moment at the window of a glove shop. She had a passion for gloves; but her own daughter Elizabeth didn't care at all for them.

Elizabeth really cared for her dog Grizzle most of all. Still, that was better than Miss Kilman! Richard said it might be only a phase which all girls go through. It might be falling in love. But why with Miss Kilman? (She *had* been badly treated, of course). Anyhow they were inseparable. Every year Miss Kilman wore that green mackintosh coat[2]; she perspired; she always made you feel her superiority, your inferiority; how poor she was; how rich you were. No doubt in another life, she would have loved Miss Kilman! But not in this world.

Nonsense, nonsense! She cried to herself, as she entered Mulberry's, the florist's — to be greeted at once by button-faced Miss Pym, whose hands were always bright red, as if they had been stood in cold water with the flowers. (She looked older this year.)

There were delphiniums, sweet peas, bunches of lilac; and carnations, masses of carnations. There were roses; there were irises. Clarissa breathed in[3] the earthy garden sweet smell as she stood

---

1. Fear no more...rages: 引自莎劇《辛白林》的輓歌:不再畏懼灼熱的太陽,或寒冬暴怒的吼叫

2. mackintosh coat: 雨衣
3. breathed in: 吸入

talking to Miss Pym. While she began to go with her from jar to jar, choosing, she said, 'Nonsense, nonsense,' to herself, more and more gently when — oh! A pistol shot in the street outside!

'Dear, those motor cars,' said Miss Pym, going to the window to look, and coming back and smiling apologetically[1], as if those tyres of motor cars were all HER fault.

The violent explosion which made Mrs Dalloway jump and Miss Pym go to the window and apologise came from a motor car which had pulled up precisely opposite Mulberry's shop window. Passers-by stopped and stared and had just enough time to see a *very* important face against the dove-grey upholstery[2], before a male hand drew the blind[3] and there was nothing more to be seen.

Yet rumours[4] were at once in circulation: was it the Prince of Wales's, the Queen's, the Prime Minister's? Whose face was it? Nobody knew.

Septimus Warren Smith, aged about thirty, pale-faced, with hazel[5] eyes, beak-nosed, wearing brown shoes and a shabby[6] overcoat, found himself unable to pass.

Everything had come to a standstill. The motor car had stopped outside Mulberry's shop window; Mrs Dalloway, with her arms full of sweet peas, looked out. Everyone looked at the motor car. Septimus looked; I am blocking the way, he thought.

'Let us go on, Septimus,' said his wife, a little Italian woman with large eyes and a pointed face.

Lucrezia herself could not help looking at the motor car. Was it the Queen in there — the Queen going shopping?

1. **apologetically:** 抱歉地
2. **upholstery:** 車內皮製座位
3. **blind:** 窗簾
4. **rumours:** 謠言
5. **hazel:** 琥珀色
6. **shabby:** 襤褸

'Come on,' said Lucrezia; but her husband (for they had been married four, five years now) jumped and said, 'All right!' angrily, as if she had interrupted him.

People must notice, she thought, looking at the crowd staring at the motor car. Septimus had said, 'I will kill myself'; suppose they had heard him? Help, help! She wanted to cry out.

'Now we will cross the road,' said Lucrezia — so simple, so impulsive, only twenty-four, without friends in England; she who had left Italy for his sake[1].

The motor car with its blinds drawn proceeded towards Piccadilly. The face itself had been seen only once by three people for a few seconds. But greatness was definitely seated inside; greatness was passing, hidden, down Bond Street. It is probably the Queen, thought Mrs Dalloway, coming out of Mulberry's with her flowers.

The traffic was terrible for the time of day; the Queen herself unable to pass. The chauffeur said or showed something to the policeman, who saluted, and the car passed through, slowly and very silently. Clarissa guessed; she had seen something white, magical, circular, in the footman's hand, a disc inscribed with a name — the Queen's, the Prince of Wales's, the Prime Minister's.

Gliding[2] across Piccadilly, the car turned down St. James's Street. A small crowd meanwhile had gathered at the gates of Buckingham Palace. The Prince lived at St. James's; but he might come along in the morning to visit his mother.

So Sarah Bletchley said, with her baby in her arms, while Emily Coates looked at the Palace windows and thought of all the housemaids, all the bedrooms. The crowd increased. Little Mr Bowley

1. for his sake: 為他着想
2. gliding: 滑過

actually had tears in his eyes. He raised his hat as the car turned into the Mall and held it high as the car approached.

Suddenly Mrs Coates looked up into the sky. An aeroplane was coming over the trees, letting out white smoke from behind, making letters in the sky! Everyone looked up.

What letters? A C was it? An E, then an L? For a moment they lay still; then they melted in the sky, and the aeroplane shot further away and again, in a fresh space of sky, and began writing a K, an E, a Y perhaps?

'Glaxo,' said Mrs Coates, looking straight up, and her baby, lying in her arms, gazed straight up.

'Kreemo,' murmured Mrs Bletchley. With his hat held out perfectly still in his hand, Mr Bowley gazed straight up. As they looked, the whole world became perfectly silent, and a flight of gulls[1] crossed the sky, and in this extraordinary silence and peace, bells struck eleven times, the sound fading[2] up there among the gulls.

The aeroplane turned and swooped[3] exactly where it liked —

'That's an E,' said Mrs Bletchley —

'It's toffee,' murmured Mr Bowley — (and the car went in at the Palace gates and nobody looked at it).

The plane shut off the smoke and rushed away. It had gone. There was no sound. The clouds to which the letters E, G, or L had attached themselves moved freely. Then suddenly, as a train comes out of a tunnel, the aeroplane rushed out of the clouds again, soared up and wrote one letter after another — but what word was it writing?

Lucrezia Warren Smith, sitting by her husband's side on a seat in Regent's Park, looked up.

---

1. **a flight of gulls:** 鷗羣
2. **fading:** 漸漸隱去
3. **swooped:** 突然撲下來

'Look, look, Septimus!' she cried. For Dr Holmes had told her to make her husband take an interest in things outside himself. So, thought Septimus, looking up, they are signalling to me. Tears filled his eyes as he looked at the smoke words melting in the sky and leaving him with shapes of unimaginable beauty! Tears ran down his cheeks.

It was toffee; they were advertising toffee, a nursemaid[1] told Rezia. Together they began to spell t... o... f...

'K... R... ' said the nursemaid, and Septimus heard her say 'Kay Arr' close to his ear, deeply, softly, but with a roughness in her voice. He shut his eyes; he would see no more.

'Septimus!' said Rezia. He started violently.

'I am going to walk to the fountain and back,' she said.

For she could stand it no longer. Dr Holmes might say there was nothing wrong with Septimus. She could not sit beside him when he stared like that and did not see her and made everything terrible. 'Septimus has been working too hard' — that was all she could say to her own mother. Looking back, she saw him sitting in his shabby overcoat alone, on the seat, staring. Septimus had fought in the War; he was brave; but he was not Septimus now. She put on her new hat and he never noticed; and he was happy without her. Nothing could make her happy without him! He was selfish, like all men. It was she who suffered — but she had nobody to tell.

Italy — with its white houses and the room where her sisters sat making hats, and the streets crowded every evening with people walking, laughing out loud — was far away.

There was nobody. Her words faded. I am alone; I am alone! She

---

1. nursemaid: 護理員

cried, by the fountain in Regent's Park. For he was gone, she thought — but no; there he was; still sitting alone on the seat, talking aloud.

'What are you saying?' said Rezia suddenly, sitting down by him.

Interrupted again! She was always interrupting.

Away from people — they must get away from people, he said (jumping up), right away over there, where there were chairs under a tree. There they sat down.

The way to Regent's Park Tube station — could they tell her the way? — Maisie Johnson wanted to know. She had only arrived from Edinburgh two days ago.

'Not this way — over there!' Rezia exclaimed, waving her away, in case she should see Septimus. Both seemed queer[1], Maisie Johnson thought.

The aeroplane! Away and away it shot[2] over Greenwich; over the little island of grey churches, St. Paul's and the rest until, on either side of London, fields spread out.

It was strange; it was still. There was no sound to be heard above the traffic. The aeroplane curved freely up and up, straight up, and white smoke poured out from behind, looping[3], writing a T, an O, an F.

1. **queer:** 奇怪的
2. **shot:** 快速地掠過
3. **looping:** 繞圈

Reading Comprehension

1 **Are these statements true (T) or false (F)?**

	T	F

1 The story of *Mrs Dalloway* takes place in late summer. ☐ ☐
2 Clarissa Dalloway is forty years old. ☐ ☐
3 Clarissa lives in one of London's central districts. ☐ ☐
4 Clarissa is thankful that she did not get married to her old friend Peter Walsh. ☐ ☐
5 Hugh Whitbread meets Clarissa in St James's Park. ☐ ☐
6 Someone fires a gun outside the florist's. ☐ ☐
7 Septimus Warren Smith is a well-dressed veteran of the First World War. ☐ ☐
8 Septimus's wife Rezia is unhappy to have left her native Italy. ☐ ☐

CAE Practice — Grammar/Vocabulary

2 **In this summary of Chapter One, put the verbs into their correct form of the past.**

On the day of her party in Westminster, Clarissa Dalloway (1) _____ (*decide*) to go to the florist's to (2) _____ (*choose*) the flowers herself. As she (3) _____ (*walk*) through the streets, she remembered a happy time at her family home when she was eighteen, and she also (4) _____ (*think*) about her old friend Peter Walsh, whom she (5) _____ _____ (*refuse*) to marry. In St James's Park, Clarissa (6) _____ (*be*) surprised to meet another old friend, Hugh Whitbread, who (7) _____ (*assure*) her that he and his wife (8) _____ _____ (*be*) at the party. While she was looking at the flowers in the shop, Clarissa (9) _____ (*hear*) a loud noise outside; a large motor-car had stopped opposite and seemed to be (10) _____ (*carry*) a very important passenger. Eventually the car (11) _____ (*drive*) away and went towards St James's. Meanwhile, Septimus Warren Smith and his Italian wife Rezia, who had seen the car, went to (12) _____ (*sit*) in Regent's Park. Rezia was unhappy because her husband just (13) _____ (*stare*) ahead of him and did not talk to her; she also (14) _____ (*realise*) that she (15) _____ (*miss*) her homeland. They and other people watched a plane (16) _____ (*fly*) above them, which (17) _____ _____ (*pour out*) white smoke to publicise a toffee product.

Text Analysis

3 **Can you identify who is speaking?**

1 'What a surprise to see you here!' _____

2 'What about some sweet peas for the tables, Mrs Dalloway?'
_____

3 'You are always interrupting!' _____

4 'Please be assured, we shall be at the party tonight.'
_____

5 'Well, that couple I've just spoken to is VERY strange!'
_____

6 'I don't recognise him any more… and I can't talk to anyone!'
_____

Note-taking

4 **In this chapter, we read Clarissa Dalloway's thoughts about her past, her present and her future. Write in her notebook below.**

Past

Present

Future

Making Sense — Grammar

5 **What do these sentences from the text mean? Rewrite them, using your own words and including the word in brackets.**

1 *'Septimus had said, 'I will kill myself'; suppose they had heard him?'*

Rezia was worried (announce) _____

_____

2 *'Dr Holmes had told her to make her husband take an interest in things outside himself.'*

Dr Holmes wanted Rezia (encourage) _____

_____

3 *'She would have preferred to be like Richard, who did things for themselves.'*

Clarissa really wanted (attitude) _____

_____

4 *'Did it matter then, she asked herself, that she must inevitably cease to exist completely; all this must go on without her?'*

Clarissa wondered whether (die) _____

_____

Reading Comprehension

6 **Focus on Septimus Warren Smith. How does he compare with Clarissa?**
Make notes for the categories in the chart below.

	Marriage	Love	Life and Death	Character
Septimus				
Clarissa				

Speaking

7 **Think about the difference between Clarissa's marriage to Richard and Septimus's to Rezia. Are there any similarities or parallels? Discuss your ideas.**

Writing

8 Imagine that you are Clarissa writing in your diary about your thoughts and what happened during the visit to Mulberry's the florist's. Use the first-person 'I' form.

PRE-READING ACTIVITIES

Speaking

9 In Chapter Two, Clarissa receives an unexpected visit from someone from her past. Who do you think this might be, and what effect will it have on her?

_____

_____

_____

Reading Comprehension

10 Guess if these statements from Chapter Two are True (T) or False (F), then check your answers.

		T	F
1	Clarissa used to sit on the floor smoking cigarettes with Sally Seton.	☐	☐
2	Clarissa was excited for Richard about his lunch appointment at Lady Bruton's.	☐	☐
3	Elizabeth Dalloway interrupted her mother's conversation with Peter Walsh.	☐	☐
4	Peter Walsh thought that Clarissa didn't look any older than when he last saw her.	☐	☐
5	Clarissa admitted to herself that she had had strong feelings for Sally at Bourton.	☐	☐
6	Clarissa was surprised when her maid Lucy told her about Mr Dalloway's lunch appointment.	☐	☐
7	Peter felt relaxed about seeing Clarissa again.	☐	☐
8	Clarissa thought that Peter had lost weight.	☐	☐

Chapter Two

An Echo from the Past

'What are they looking at?' said Clarissa Dalloway to the maid who opened her door.

The hall of the house was cool. Mrs Dalloway heard the swish[1] of Lucy's skirts. The cook whistled in the kitchen. She heard the click of the typewriter. It was her life; she felt blessed[2] and purified. Meanwhile Lucy stood by her, trying to explain how

'Mr Dalloway, ma'am'—

Clarissa took the telephone pad and read, 'Lady Bruton wishes to know if Mr Dalloway will lunch with her to-day.'

'Mr Dalloway, ma'am, told me to tell you he would be lunching out.'

'Dear!' said Clarissa, and Lucy shared her disappointment, as she intended her to.

'Fear no more,' said Clarissa. Fear no more the heat o' the sun; the shock of Lady Bruton asking Richard to lunch without her made her shiver[3]. Millicent Bruton, whose lunch parties were said to be extraordinarily amusing, had not asked her. No vulgar jealousy could separate her from Richard.

She put the pad on the hall table. She began to go slowly upstairs, with her hand on the bannisters[4]. She paused by the open staircase

1. **swish:** 嗖嗖聲
2. **blessed:** 幸福
3. **shiver:** 顫抖
4. **bannisters:** 樓梯扶手

window which let in blinds flapping[1], dogs barking, the flowering of the day. She felt herself suddenly aged; Lady Bruton, whose lunch parties were said to be extraordinarily amusing, had not asked her.

She came to the bathroom. There was an emptiness about the heart of life; an attic room. She laid her yellow hat on the bed. The sheets were clean, the candle was half burnt down and she had read late at night. For the House[2] sat so long that Richard insisted, after her illness, that she must sleep undisturbed. So the room was an attic; the bed narrow; she slept badly. Lying awake, the floor creaked; the lit house was suddenly darkened, and if she raised her head she could just hear the click of the handle released as gently as possible by Richard, who crept upstairs in his socks and then usually dropped his hot-water bottle and swore[3]! How she laughed!

But this question of love (she thought, putting her coat away), this falling in love with women. Take Sally Seton; her relation in the old days with Sally Seton. After all, had that not been love?

She sat on the floor — that was her first impression of Sally — her arms round her knees, smoking a cigarette. Where could it have been? At some party; she had a vague memory of saying to the man she was with, 'Who is THAT?' And he had told her, and said that Sally's parents did not get on[4] (how that shocked her — that one's parents should quarrel!). But all that evening she could not take her eyes off Sally, her extraordinary beauty, dark, large-eyed, with that quality of abandonment, as if she could say anything, do anything; a quality much commoner in foreigners than in Englishwomen. Sally always said she had French blood in her. That summer she came unexpectedly to stay at Bourton, walking in one night after dinner,

1. flapping: 隨風飄揚
2. the House: 下議院

3. swore: 說粗言穢語
4. get on: 相處融洽

and upsetting poor Aunt Helena, who never forgave her. There had been a quarrel at home and she had rushed off in a passion. She and Clarissa sat up talking till all hours of the night. Sally was the first person to make her feel how sheltered[1] life at Bourton was. She knew nothing about sex — nothing about social problems. They sat, hour after hour, talking in her bedroom at the top of the house, talking about life, how they were to reform the world.

Sally's power was her gift, her personality. There was her way with flowers, for instance. At Bourton they always had stiff little vases all the way down the table. Sally went out, picked all sorts of flowers never seen together — then she cut their heads off, and made them swim on the top of water in bowls. The effect was extraordinary — coming in to dinner in the sunset.

The strange thing, looking back, was the purity, the integrity, of her feeling for Sally. It was not like one's feeling for a man. It was completely disinterested; it had a quality which could only exist between women just grown up. It was protective, on her side; it came from a feeling of being in league[2] together, aware that something would inevitably separate them (they spoke of marriage always as a catastrophe).

Now Clarissa could not even get an echo of her old emotion. But she could remember going cold with excitement, doing her hair in a kind of ecstasy[3], dressing and going downstairs, and feeling as Othello felt: 'if it were now to die 'twere now to be most happy[4].'

But nothing is so strange when one is in love (and what was this except being in love?) as the complete indifference of other people. Aunt Helena just wandered off[5] after dinner; Papa read the paper. Peter

---

1. **sheltered:** 受到保護
2. **being in league:** 結為同盟
3. **ecstasy:** 狂喜
4. **if it were...happy:** 摘自莎劇《奧賽羅》：如果即將要死去，那此刻就是最快樂的時光
5. **wandered off:** 漫步

Walsh might have been there. Sally stood by the fireplace talking, in that beautiful voice, to Papa, when suddenly she said, 'What a shame to sit indoors!' and they all went out on to the terrace. Then came the most exquisite moment of her whole life: Sally stopped and picked a flower; kissed her on the lips. The whole world might have turned upside down! The others disappeared; there she was alone with Sally. And she felt that she had been given a present, wrapped up, and told just to keep it, not to look at it.

Laying her brooch on the table, she had a sudden spasm[1]. She was not old yet. She had just broken into her fifty-second year. Clarissa crossed to the dressing-table and saw in the mirror the delicate pink face of the woman who was that same night to give a party; of Clarissa Dalloway; of herself.

Her evening dresses hung in the cupboard. Clarissa gently detached the green one and carried it to the window. She had torn it. Someone had trod on[2] the skirt at the Embassy party. She would take it down into the drawing-room and mend it, and wear it tonight.

Strange, she thought, pausing on the landing, how she knew the temper of her own house! Faint[3] sounds came up the stairs: the cleaning of a floor; knocking; the front door opening loudly; a voice repeating a message in the basement; clean silver on a tray for the party. All was for the party. (And Lucy, coming into the drawing-room with her tray held out, put the giant candlesticks on the mantelpiece[4]. The guests would come; they would stand; they would talk in the mincing[5] tones of ladies and gentlemen. But her mistress was the loveliest of all of them — and here she was, coming in!)

'Oh Lucy,' Mrs Dalloway said, 'the silver does look nice!' She took

1. **spasm:** 抽筋
2. **trod on:** 踩到
3. **faint:** 遠處的
4. **mantelpiece:** 壁爐架
5. **mincing:** 矯揉造作

the old cushion in the middle of the sofa, put it in Lucy's arms and gave her a little push, crying: 'Take it away!'

Lucy stopped at the drawing-room door, holding the cushion, and said, very shyly, turning a little pink, Couldn't she help to mend that dress?

But, said Mrs Dalloway, she had enough on her hands[1] already. 'But, thank you, Lucy,' said Mrs Dalloway, sitting down on the sofa with her dress over her knees, her scissors. She went on saying thank you in gratitude to her servants generally for helping her to be what she wanted, gentle, generous-hearted. Her servants liked her. And then this dress of hers — where was the tear? This was a favourite dress.

Quiet descended on her, calm, content, as her needle did the work; just like on a summer's day waves collect, overbalance[2], and fall. And the body alone listens to the passing bee; the wave breaking; the dog barking far away.

'Heavens, the front-door bell!' exclaimed Clarissa. She stopped and listened.

'Mrs Dalloway will see me,' said the elderly man in the hall. 'Oh yes, she will see ME,' he repeated, putting Lucy aside very benevolently, and running upstairs ever so quickly. 'Yes, yes, yes,' he muttered as he ran upstairs. 'She will see me. After five years in India, Clarissa will see me.'

'Who can — what can,' asked Mrs Dalloway (thinking it was unacceptable to be interrupted at eleven o'clock on the morning of the day she was giving a party). She heard a hand upon the door; she tried to hide her dress. Now the door opened, and in came —

---

1. **on her hands:** 手頭上（要完成的工作）
2. **collect, overbalance:** 聚集，失去平衡

for a single second she could not remember what he was called! So surprised she was to see him, so glad, so shy, so shocked to have Peter Walsh come to her unexpectedly in the morning!

'And how are you?' said Peter Walsh, trembling; taking her hand; kissing her hand. She's grown older, he thought, sitting down, but I shan't tell her. She's looking at me, he thought, suddenly embarrassed, though he had kissed her hands. Putting his hand into his pocket, he took out a large pocket-knife and half opened the blade.

Exactly the same, thought Clarissa; the same strange look; a little thinner, perhaps, but he looks very well.

'How wonderful to see you again!' she exclaimed. He had his knife out. That's just like him, she thought.

He had only reached London last night, he said; he would have to go to the country at once; and how was everything, how was everybody — Richard? Elizabeth?

'And what's all this?' he said, moving his pen-knife towards her green dress.

He's very well dressed, thought Clarissa; yet he always criticises ME.

Here she is, mending her dress, as usual, he thought; she's been sitting here all the time I've been in India — mending her dress, going to parties; running to the House and back, he thought, growing more and more irritated and agitated, for there's nothing in the world so bad for some women as marriage, he thought; and politics; and having a Conservative husband, like the admirable Richard. He shut his knife with a snap.

'Richard's very well. Richard's at a Committee[1],' said Clarissa.

1. Committee: 委員會

And she opened her scissors, and said, did he mind her just finishing what she was doing to her dress, for they had a party that night? 'Which I shan't ask you to, my dear Peter!' she said.

How delicious to hear her say that — my dear Peter! Why wouldn't she ask him to her party?

Now of course, thought Clarissa, he's so charming! Now I remember how impossible it was to make up my mind, that awful summer, not to marry him — and why did I make up my mind, she wondered?

'But it's extraordinary that you came this morning!' she cried.

Peter moved a little towards Clarissa; put his hand out; raised it; let it fall.

Why go back like this to the past? he thought.

Clarissa looked at Peter Walsh; her look, passing through all that time and that emotion, reached him doubtfully; settled on him tearfully; and then flew away like a bird. Quite simply she wiped her eyes.

Stop! Stop! Peter wanted to cry. For he was not old; his life was not over; he was only just past fifty. Shall I tell her, he thought, or not? But she is too cold, he thought; sewing, with her scissors; Daisy would look ordinary beside Clarissa. And she would think me a failure, which I am in their sense, he thought; in the Dalloways' sense. He took out his knife quite openly — his old horn-handled knife which Clarissa was sure he had had these thirty years — and held it tightly.

What an extraordinary habit that was, Clarissa thought; always playing with a knife. This visit had surprised her — it had upset her. She thought of all the things she did: the things she liked; her husband; Elizabeth; herself, which Peter hardly knew now.

'Well, and what's happened to you?' she said. So Peter Walsh and Clarissa, sitting side by side on the blue sofa, challenged each other. 'Millions of things!' he exclaimed, and raised his hands to his forehead.

Clarissa sat very upright; drew in her breath.

'I am in love,' he said, speaking rather dryly to Clarissa Dalloway; 'in love with a girl in India.'

'In love!' she said. At his age! She thought. His hands are red; and he's six months older than I am! But in her heart she felt, he is in love. Not with her. With some younger woman, of course.

'And who is she?' she asked.

'A married woman, unfortunately,' he said. 'She has two small children; a boy and a girl; and I have come over to see my lawyers about the divorce.'

'But what are you going to do?' she asked him. Oh the lawyers and solicitors[1] were going to do it, he said. Then to his complete surprise, he burst into tears; wept without the least shame, sitting on the sofa, the tears running down his cheeks.

And Clarissa had leant forward, taken his hand, drawn him to her, kissed him, — actually had felt his face on hers and thinking suddenly, 'If I had married him, this gaiety[2] would have been mine all day! Richard, Richard!' She cried, as a sleeper in the night starts and stretches a hand in the dark for help. Lunching with Lady Bruton, it came back to her. He has left me; I am alone forever, she thought, folding her hands upon her knee.

Peter Walsh had got up and crossed to the window and stood with his back to her. Take me with you, Clarissa thought impulsively, as

1. **solicitors:** （英式英語）律師
2. **gaiety:** 喜悦

if he were starting directly upon some great voyage; and then, next moment, it was over. She rose from the sofa and went to Peter.

'Tell me,' he said, seizing her by the shoulders. 'Are you happy, Clarissa? Does Richard —'

The door opened.

'Here is my Elizabeth,' said Clarissa, emotionally, histrionically[1], perhaps.

'How d'y do?' said Elizabeth coming forward; then Big Ben struck, vigorously.

'Hullo, Elizabeth!' cried Peter, going quickly to her, saying 'Good-bye, Clarissa' without looking at her, leaving the room quickly, and running downstairs and opening the hall door.

'Peter! Peter!' cried Clarissa, following him out on to the landing. 'My party tonight! Remember my party tonight!' she cried, having to raise her voice against the roar[2] of the open air. With the traffic and the sound of all the clocks striking, her voice crying, 'Remember my party tonight!' sounded frail[3] and thin and very far away as Peter Walsh shut the door.

---

1. **histrionically:** 矯揉造作地
2. **roar:** 低沉的吼叫聲
3. **frail:** 脆弱

AFTER-READING ACTIVITIES

Grammar

1 **Look at these examples from Chapter Two and, as in the example below, re-write them in direct speech.**

> She would take the dress down into the drawing-room and mend it.
> _Clarissa said, 'I'll take the dress down into the drawing-room_
> _and mend it.'_

1 Lucy said, very shyly, Couldn't she help to mend that dress?

_____

2 But, said Mrs Dalloway, she had enough on her hands already.

_____

3 He had only reached London last night, Peter said; he would have to go to the country at once...

_____

4 Clarissa said, did Peter mind her just finishing what she was doing to her dress, for they had a party that night?

_____

5 The lawyers and solicitors were going to do it, Peter said.

_____

Vocabulary

2 **Compare the characters of Clarissa and Sally Seton. Write words and phrases in the chart below.**

CLARISSA	SALLY

Text Analysis

3 **Can you identify who is speaking, and what happens next?**

1 'What a shame to sit indoors!'

_____

2 'Yes, yes, yes. She will see me.'

_____

3 'How d'y do?'

_____

4 'Mr Dalloway, ma'am'

_____

5 '... the silver does look nice!'

_____

Grammar

4 **Use these key words to make complete sentences. Think carefully about the verbs — and you might have to add a word or two!**

1 Lady / realise / when / Bruton / try / Clarissa / (not) be / that / disappointed / invite / lunch / (not) feel / she / she

2 fall in love / wonder / with / about / Clarissa / the / man / difference / with / woman / a / a / and

3 stairs / party / Clarissa / top / stop / the / her / preparations / of / listen / the / to / to / the

4 eyes / could (not) / room / the / Walsh / believe / Peter / friend /come / when / her / old / Clarissa

5 irritated / Clarissa / situation / Peter / lifestyle / become / more / because / her / more / and / and

6 Elizabeth / Clarissa / room / Peter / conversation / run / the / interrupt / when / his

Making Sense of the Text

5 **Look at these examples from the text and think about what they mean at each point in the story.**

1 There was an emptiness about the heart of life: an attic room.

_____

_____

2 ... her look, passing through all that time and that emotion, reached him doubtfully ...

_____

_____

3 'But what are you going to do?' she asked him.

_____

_____

4 She had just broken into her fifty-second year.

_____

_____

5 ... her extraordinary beauty ... with that quality of abandonment ... much commoner in foreigners than in Englishwomen.

_____

_____

PRE-READING ACTIVITIES

Reading Comprehension

6 **Look at these statements about what happens in Chapter Three and decide if they are True (T), False (F). Then check your answers.**

		T	F
1	Peter decides to go to Clarissa's party.	☐	☐
2	Peter thinks about Clarissa and is happy that she refused to marry him.	☐	☐
3	Peter wanted the woman he was following to talk to him.	☐	☐

4 When he is sitting in Regent's Park, Peter does not mind if people ask him the time. ☐☐

5 Peter's dream is about his experiences with women throughout his life. ☐☐

6 At Bourton, Peter never thought that Clarissa would one day marry Richard. ☐☐

7 When Clarissa and Peter talked on the island, Clarissa forgot about Richard. ☐☐

8 Peter felt ashamed at having wept at Clarissa's house. ☐☐

Vocabulary

7 **Look at these adjectives. Match each one with a character from Chapter Three, like the example.**

	CLARISSA	RICHARD	PETER	THE WOMAN	ELIZABETH
arrogant					
attractive					
awkward					
big					
cold					
delightful					
emotional					
empty					
enchanting					
grown-up					
handsome					
happy					
hard					
insincere					
maternal					
sad					
sentimental	✓				
strange-looking					
unimaginative					
young					

Chapter Three

Painful Memories

▶ 3 Remember my party, remember my party, said Peter Walsh as he stepped down the street, speaking to himself rhythmically, in time with Big Ben striking the half-hour. Why does Clarissa give these parties, he thought. He did not blame her. Only one person in the world could be as he was, in love, really for the first time in his life. Clarissa had grown hard, he thought; and a little sentimental, too, he suspected.

The way she said 'Here is my Elizabeth!' annoyed him. Why not 'Here's Elizabeth' simply? It was insincere. And Elizabeth didn't like it either. There was always something cold in Clarissa, he thought. She had always, even as a girl, a sort of timidity, which in middle age becomes conventionality[1]. He wondered whether by calling[2] at that hour he had annoyed her; overcome with shame suddenly at having been a fool; wept; been emotional; told her everything, as usual.

As a cloud crosses the sun, silence falls on London; and falls on the mind. Peter Walsh felt hollowed out[3], completely empty within. Clarissa refused me, he thought. He stood there thinking, Clarissa refused me.

From behind came a regular sound, strict in step[4], up Whitehall. Boys in uniform, carrying guns, marched, their arms stiff, and on

1. conventionality: 世俗
2. calling: 探望

3. hollowed out: 掏空
4. strict in step: 腳步規整

their faces an expression like the letters of a legend written round the base of a statue praising duty, gratitude, fidelity[1], love of England.

It is a very fine training, thought Peter Walsh, as he began to keep step with them. But they did not look robust[2]. They were mostly boys of sixteen. I can't keep up with them[3], Peter Walsh thought, as they marched up Whitehall, and they marched past him and past everyone. And just because nobody yet knew he was in London, except Clarissa, the strangeness of standing alone, alive, unknown, at half-past eleven in Trafalgar Square overcame him. I haven't felt so young for years! thought Peter, feeling like a child who runs out of doors, and sees, as he runs, his old nurse waving at the wrong window.

As he walked across Trafalgar Square, he noticed a young woman. She's extraordinarily attractive, he thought, walking in the direction of the Haymarket; young, but stately; merry, but discreet[4]; black, but enchanting. Peter started following with excitement. 'You,' she seemed to say; the wind made her thin long cloak[5] blow out tenderly, like arms opening and taking the tired —

But she's not married; she's quite young, thought Peter. She waited at the kerbstone. There was a dignity about her. She was not worldly[6], not rich, like Clarissa. Was she, he wondered, respectable? She moved; she crossed; he followed her. To embarrass her was the last thing he wanted. But if she stopped, he would say, 'Come and have an ice,' and she would answer, perfectly simply, 'Oh yes.'

But other people got between them in the street. She went on, across Piccadilly, and up Regent Street, ahead of him, her cloak, her gloves, her shoulders. Laughing and delightful, she had crossed Oxford Street and Great Portland Street and turned down one of the

---

1. **fidelity:** 忠誠
2. **robust:** 強壯
3. **keep up with them:** 跟上他們

4. **merry, but discreet:** 歡快但不張揚
5. **cloak:** 斗篷
6. **worldly:** 世故

little streets, and now she slowed down, opened her bag, and with one look in his direction, but not at him, one look that said goodbye for ever, she fitted her key, opened the door, and was gone! Clarissa's voice saying, Remember my party, sang in his ears. It was over.

Well, I've had my fun, he thought, looking up at the hanging baskets of pale geraniums; his invented fun with the girl. He turned; went up the street, thinking to find somewhere to sit, till it was time for Lincoln's Inn — for the solicitors. Where should he go? No matter[1]. Up the street, then, towards Regent's Park.

It was a splendid morning too. Life struck straight[2] through the streets. London was splendid in its own way; the season; civilisation. Coming from a respectable Anglo-Indian family, there were moments when civilisation seemed dear to him, like a personal possession; everything was really very tolerable; and he would sit down in the shade and smoke.

There was Regent's Park. Yes. As a child he had walked in Regent's Park — it was strange, he thought, how the thought of childhood keeps coming back to me — the result of seeing Clarissa, perhaps; for women live much more in the past than we do, he thought. They attach themselves to places.

Yes, he remembered Regent's Park; the long straight walk. He looked for an empty seat. He did not want to be bothered by people asking him the time. An elderly grey nurse, with a baby asleep in its pram — the best he could do for himself was to sit down at the far end of the seat by that nurse.

Peter suddenly remembered Elizabeth as she came into the room and stood by her mother. She's strange-looking, he thought; big,

1. **no matter:** 小事而已
2. **struck straight:** 直接衝擊

quite grown-up, handsome rather than pretty; and she can't be more than eighteen. Probably she doesn't get on with Clarissa. 'There's my Elizabeth,' Clarissa had said — why not 'Here's Elizabeth' simply?

The rich cigar smoke flowed coolly down his throat. I shall try and speak to Elizabeth alone tonight, he thought. He quickly closed his eyes, raised his hand and threw away the end of his cigar. Children's voices, people passing, rising and falling traffic, all swept across his mind; he sank into sleep and began snoring, as the grey nurse resumed her knitting.

To Peter sleeping, the grey nurse seems like a vision from the forest made of sky and branches. Peter dreams of the solitary traveller journeying through a forest. Nothing exists outside us, the traveller thinks, except a state of mind, a desire for comfort, for relief. The sky and branches become a woman; the solitary traveller experiences other visions, which take away from him the sense of the earth and instead give him a general peace in the simplicity of life. Now the traveller is old, over fifty; and from the hands of the woman come compassion, comprehension and absolution. Soon the solitary traveller leaves the forest and comes to a door with shaded eyes; he meets an elderly woman who seems to be looking for a lost son, like the figure of the mother whose sons have been killed in the battles of the world. The traveller moves down the village street; the evening seems ominous[1]; everyone seems to be waiting for the end. Suddenly a cupboard, a table, a window with flowers, and the outline of Mrs Turner, Peter's landlady, bending down to remove the tablecloth and putting the marmalade[2] away in the cupboard. 'There is nothing more tonight, sir?'

1. **ominous:** 不祥
2. **marmalade:** 柑橘醬

But who does the solitary traveller reply to?

As the elderly nurse knitted, over the sleeping baby in Regent's Park, Peter Walsh snored.

After a while, he woke with extreme suddenness, saying to himself, 'The death of the soul.' 'Lord, Lord!' he said to himself out loud, stretching and opening his eyes. 'The death of the soul.' The words attached themselves to some scene, to some room, to some past he had been dreaming of. It became clearer; the scene, the room, the past he had been dreaming of: Bourton, that summer, early in the 1890s, when he was so passionately in love with Clarissa. Many people were there, laughing and talking, sitting round a table. They were talking about a man who had married his housemaid, and she had been brought to Bourton for what was an awful visit. She was absurdly over-dressed, 'like a cockatoo[1],' Clarissa had said, imitating her, and she never stopped talking. Then Sally Seton said, did it make any real difference to one's feelings to know that before they'd married she had had a baby? Clarissa turned bright pink and said, 'Oh, I shall never be able to speak to her again!' And everything became very uncomfortable.

It was Clarissa's manner that annoyed Peter; timid; hard; arrogant; unimaginative. 'The death of the soul' — the death of her soul. Then Clarissa, offended with them all, got up, made some excuse, and went off, alone. As she opened the door, her big sheepdog came in — and she threw herself upon him enthusiastically. It was as if she was saying to Peter, 'I know you thought my reaction about that woman was absurd, but see how sympathetic[2] I am; see how I love my Rob!'

Strangely, they had always communicated without words. She

1. **cockatoo:** 鳳頭鸚鵡
2. **sympathetic:** 富同情心

knew that he criticised her; then she would do something quite obvious to defend herself, but he was never convinced. He just said nothing and looked sad. That was the way their quarrels often began.

It was an awful evening! He grew more and more pessimistic about everything. And he couldn't see her to explain, because there were always people about. She pretended nothing had happened. That was the devilish part of her — this coldness, something very profound in her, which he had felt again this morning talking to her; an impenetrability[1]. Yet Heaven knows he loved her.

He had gone in to dinner rather late, and had sat down beside Clarissa's Aunt Helena, and couldn't speak. Then half-way through dinner he made himself look across at Clarissa for the first time. She was talking to a young man on her right. He had a sudden revelation. 'She will marry that man,' he said to himself. He didn't even know his name.

For of course it was that afternoon that Dalloway had come over; and Clarissa got his name wrong and introduced him to everybody as 'Wickham'. At last he said, 'My name is Dalloway!'— that was his first view of Richard — a fair young man, rather awkward, sitting on a deck-chair[2], and shouting, 'My name is Dalloway!' Clarissa's manner with him was — how could he describe it? — easy; maternal; gentle. They were talking about politics. All through dinner he tried to hear what they were saying.

Afterwards Clarissa came up to him, like a real hostess, and wanted to introduce him to someone. She spoke to Peter as if they had never met before, which made him angry. But he admired her courage; her social instinct. 'The perfect hostess,' he said to her, and he wanted

1. **impenetrability:** 不可穿透
2. **deck-chair:** 躺椅

her to feel it. He would have done anything to hurt her after seeing her with Dalloway. So she left him. Never, never had he suffered so infernally[1]! People began going out of the room. They were going boating on the lake by moonlight — one of Sally's mad ideas. He could hear her describing the moon. And they all went out. He was left quite alone.

'Don't you want to go with them?' said Aunt Helena. And he turned round and there was Clarissa again. She had come back to fetch him. He was overcome by her generosity — her goodness.

'Come along,' she said. 'They're waiting.' He had never felt so happy in the whole of his life! Without a word they were friends again. They walked down to the lake. He had twenty minutes of perfect happiness. Her voice, her spirit, her adventurousness; she made everyone explore the island; she laughed; she sang. And all the time, he knew, Dalloway was falling in love with her; she was falling in love with Dalloway; but it didn't seem to matter. Nothing mattered. They sat on the ground and talked — he and Clarissa. They went in and out of each other's minds without any effort[2]. And then in a second it was over. He said to himself as they were getting into the boat, 'She will marry that man', without any resentment[3]; but it was an obvious thing. Dalloway would marry Clarissa.

Dalloway rowed everyone back in the boat. He said nothing — but he obviously did feel, instinctively, tremendously[4], strongly, the night; the romance; Clarissa. He deserved to have her.

Peter now realised that his demands upon Clarissa were absurd. He asked impossible things. He made terrible scenes. Clarissa would have accepted him still, perhaps, if he had been less absurd. Sally

---

1. **infernally:** 極為痛苦地
2. **without any effort:** 不費吹灰之力
3. **resentment:** 恨意
4. **tremendously:** 極其、非常

thought so; she told him in long letters which she wrote to him all that summer. How she and Clarissa had talked of him; how Sally had praised him, and how Clarissa had burst into tears! It was an extraordinary summer at Bourton — all letters, scenes, telegrams — talking to Sally in the vegetable garden; Clarissa in bed with headaches.

The final scene, the terrible scene which he believed had mattered more than anything in the whole of his life, happened at three o'clock in the afternoon on a very hot day. Something small had preceded[1] it — Sally at lunch saying something about Dalloway, and calling him 'My name is Dalloway'; Clarissa suddenly turning red with embarrassment and saying, 'We've had enough of that ridiculous joke.' For Peter that meant, 'I've an understanding with Richard Dalloway.' So he took it. He had not slept for nights. 'It's got to be finished one way or the other,' he said to himself. He sent a note to her by Sally asking her to meet him by the fountain at three. 'Something very important has happened,' he wrote at the end of it.

The fountain was in the middle of a little shrubbery[2], far from the house, with shrubs and trees all round it. Clarissa came there, even before the time, and they stood with the fountain between them, water dribbling[3] all the time.

She did not move. 'Tell me the truth, tell me the truth,' he kept on saying. She seemed petrified[4]. She did not move. 'Tell me the truth,' he repeated. He felt that he was grinding[5] against something physically hard; she was unyielding[6]. She was like iron, rigid up the backbone. And when she said, 'It's no use. This is the end'— after he had spoken for hours, it seemed, with tears running down his cheeks — it was

---

1. **preceded:** 在前面
2. **shrubbery:** 灌木叢
3. **dribbling:** 滴下
4. **petrified:** 驚恐
5. **grinding:** 磨擦
6. **unyielding:** 不肯屈服

as if she had hit him in the face. She turned, she left him, went away.

'Clarissa!' he cried. 'Clarissa!' But she never came back. It was over. He went away that night. He never saw her again.

Grammar

1 **Look at these examples from Chapter Three and re-write them in indirect speech, using the verb in CAPITALS.**

Why does Clarissa give these parties, he thought. WONDER
Peter wondered why Clarissa gave those parties.

1 Elizabeth's strange-looking, Peter thought, and she can't be more than eighteen. DECIDE

2 Sally Seton said, did it make any real difference to one's feelings to know that before they'd married she had had a baby? ASK

3 'She will marry that man,' Peter said to himself. BE CONVINCED

4 'Tell me the truth, tell me the truth,' Peter kept on saying to Clarissa. INSIST

5 Clarissa said to Peter, 'It's no use. This is the end'. TELL

6 I shall try and speak to Elizabeth alone tonight. MAKE UP YOUR MIND

Reading Comprehension

2 **Here are some quotes from the chapter. What or who do they refer to and what is the message behind them?**

1 ... a sort of timidity, which in middle age becomes conventionality.

2 She moved; she crossed; he followed her. To embarrass her was the last thing he wanted.

_____

_____

3 ... for women live much more in the past than we do ... They attach themselves to places.

_____

_____

4 ... nothing exists outside us ... except a state of mind, a desire for comfort, for relief.

_____

_____

5 ... her big sheepdog came in — and she threw herself upon him enthusiastically.

_____

_____

6 ... he admired her courage; her social instinct.

_____

_____

7 He had never felt so happy in the whole of his life!

_____

_____

8 ... the terrible scene which he believed had mattered more than anything in the whole of his life...

_____

_____

Vocabulary

3 Which word is the odd one out. Circle your answer.

1 speak   weep   think   remember   wonder

2 stand   walk   march   run   feel   follow

3 communicate   explain   move   talk   describe   realise

Reading Comprehension

4 Are these statements true (T) or false (F)?

		T	F
1	Peter feels upset because he was so emotional with Clarissa.	☐	☐
2	Nobody knows that Peter has come back to London.	☐	☐
3	Peter wants to ask the young woman he is following to lunch.	☐	☐
4	Peter comes from a respectable Anglo-Indian family.	☐	☐
5	Sitting on a bench in Regent's Park, Peter starts talking to a nurse.	☐	☐
6	Clarissa and Peter had always understood each other without needing to speak.	☐	☐
7	As a young man, Peter was very much in love with Clarissa, even though they argued.	☐	☐
8	After Peter had spoken to Clarissa at the fountain, she hit him in the face.	☐	☐

Making Sense

5 These sentences describe some of the action in Chapter Three. Can you put them in the correct order?

A ☐ Peter sits next to an elderly nurse, who is looking after a baby.

B ☐ Peter thinks about Clarissa's life as a hostess.

C ☐ Peter falls asleep and dreams about a solitary traveller.

D ☐ A group of teenage boys marches past.

E ☐ A cloud crosses the sun and London falls silent.

F ☐ A young woman walks towards the Haymarket.

G ☐ Peter thinks that Clarissa probably does not get on with her daughter.

H ☐ Peter finds somewhere to sit and smoke.

Grammar

6 **Here is a summary of Chapter Three, but the verbs are wrong! Correct them.**

Peter Walsh is leaving Clarissa's house and had wondered why Clarissa will spend her time to give parties. He has believed that she has been becoming conventional in her middle age. He also feel embarrassed about weep at Clarissa's.

A group of teenage boys marching past him and he is trying to keeping up with them. Then he is seeing a beautiful young woman and decided to following her. When she is going inside her house, Peter walk to Regent's Park to have found a bench on which to be relax. He fall asleep. He waked up and thinking about the time at Bourton when Clarissa will reject him.

PRE-READING ACTIVITIES

Vocabulary

7 **Think of adjectives and phrases to describe Septimus and organise them into the two categories in the chart. Then check your answers in Chapter Four.**

BEFORE THE WAR	AFTER THE WAR

Speaking

8 **In this chapter, we find out that Rezia has asked for medical help for Septimus. What do you think the doctor's reaction will be, and why?**

Chapter Four

Taking Hold of Experience

It was awful, he cried, awful, awful!

Still, the sun was hot. Still, one got over things. Still, he thought, presumably there were compensations.

But Lucrezia Warren Smith was saying to herself, It's wicked[1]; why should I suffer? No; I can't stand[2] it any longer, she was saying, having left Septimus, who wasn't Septimus any longer, to say cruel things, to talk to himself, on the seat over there.

For herself she had done nothing wrong; she had loved Septimus; she had been happy; she had had a beautiful home, and her sisters lived there still, making hats. Why should SHE suffer?

She must go back again to Septimus, since it was almost time for them to be going to Sir William Bradshaw. She must go back and tell him, go back to him sitting there on the green chair under the tree, talking to himself, or to his dead friend Evans, killed in the War.

Everyone gives up something when they marry. She had given up her home. She had come to live in this awful city. But Septimus had grown stranger and stranger. He said people were talking behind the bedroom walls. He saw things too. She could stand it no longer. She would go back to Milan.

Dr Holmes said there was nothing the matter with him. Why had

1. **wicked:** 邪惡
2. **stand:** 忍受

he moved away, then, when she sat by him? Why did he point at her hand, take it and look at it terrified?

Was it that she had taken off her wedding ring? 'My hand has grown so thin,' she said. 'I have put the ring in my purse,' she told him.

He dropped her hand. Their marriage was over, he thought, with agony[1], with relief[2]. He, Septimus, was alone.

'I am so unhappy, Septimus,' said Rezia. 'What is the time?'

'I will tell you the time,' said Septimus, very slowly, smiling mysteriously.

And that is being young, Peter Walsh thought as he passed them. To be having an awful scene — the poor girl looked absolutely desperate — in the middle of a fine summer morning. But what was it about, he wondered?

Those five years away in India — 1918 to 1923 — had been, he suspected, somehow very important. People looked different. On board ship coming home there were lots of young men and girls carrying on[3] quite openly; one girl, Betty, said she would get married when it was the right time; to some rich man and they would live in a large house near Manchester.

Who was it now who had done that? Peter Walsh asked himself, turning into the Broad Walk — married a rich man and lived in a large house near Manchester? It was Sally Seton, of course — the wild, daring, romantic Sally!

Of all Clarissa's friends, Sally was probably the best. She saw through the admirable Hugh Whitbread anyhow. He thinks of nothing but his own appearance, she said. He remembered an

1. **agony:** 劇痛
2. **relief:** 欣慰
3. **carrying on:** 對彼此感興趣

argument one Sunday morning at Bourton about women's rights. Sally suddenly lost her temper and told Hugh that he represented all that was most detestable[1] in British middle-class life. Hugh looked horrified! She detested him for some reason; she had something against him. Something had happened in the smoking-room. Hugh had insulted her — kissed her? Incredible! Nobody believed a word against Hugh of course. Who could? Kissing Sally in the smoking-room! Hugh might have kissed some Honourable Lady, perhaps; but not that penniless Sally Seton.

Hugh was the greatest snob Peter had ever met. He'd married his Honourable Evelyn; got some little job at Court[2], looking after the King's cellars! And they lived near here, he thought (looking at the pompous[3] houses overlooking the Park) — he had lunched there once. Linen cupboards, pillow-cases, old oak furniture, pictures — and Mrs Hugh, a mouse-like little woman who would suddenly say something quite unexpected and sharp.

Peter, fifty-three, two years older than Hugh, was after[4] a job. He had to come and ask him (or Dalloway) to put him into some secretary's office, to find him some job teaching little boys Latin; for if he married Daisy, even with his pension, they could never survive on less than five hundred pounds a year.

He remembered a garden at Bourton where they used to walk, and Sally laughing and begging him to save Clarissa from Hugh Whitbread and Richard Dalloway and all the other 'perfect gentlemen' who would suffocate[5] her and make her simply into a hostess. But one must do Clarissa justice[6]. She knew exactly what she wanted; she was a far better judge of character than Sally; and she had that

1. **detestable:** 可憎的
2. **Court:** 王室內府
3. **pompous:** 浮華的
4. **after:** 尋找
5. **suffocate:** 限制
6. **do...justice:** 公平對待

extraordinary gift, that woman's gift, of making a world of her own wherever she happened to be. She came into a room; she stood, as he had often seen her, in a doorway with lots of people round her. But it was Clarissa one remembered. There she was.

No, no, no! He was not in love with her any more! He only felt, after seeing her that morning, getting ready for the party, unable to get away from the thought of her. She was worldly; she was too concerned with social position and getting on in the world. These parties, for example, were all for Richard, or for her *idea* of him (he would have been happier farming in Norfolk!). Strangely, she was one of the most sceptical[1] people he had ever met; the thought that if you behaved like a lady, the Gods — who never lost a chance of spoiling[2] human lives — would be seriously disturbed. That phase came directly after Sylvia's death — that horrible affair[3]. Clarissa always said that to see your own sister killed by a falling tree, before your very eyes, was enough to make you bitter. Later she would decide that there were *no* Gods; no one was to blame; and so started doing good for the sake of goodness. And of course she enjoyed life immensely.

The compensation of growing old, Peter Walsh thought, coming out of Regent's Park, and holding his hat in hand, was simply this; that the passions remain as strong as ever, but one has gained[4] — at last!— the power which adds the supreme flavour to existence,— the power of taking hold of experience, of turning it round, slowly, in the light.

Now, at the age of fifty-three, Peter confessed, one hardly needed people any more. Life itself was enough. For hours, for days at a time, he never thought of Daisy. So could it be that he was in love with her

1. **sceptical:** 抱懷疑態度
2. **spoiling:** 破壞

3. **affair:** 事件
4. **gained:** 獲得、贏得

then, if he remembered the passion and misery of the old days? This time, however, it was completely different — and much pleasanter — because Daisy was in love with HIM. But then bursting into tears this morning, what was all that about? What could Clarissa have thought of him? A fool presumably, not for the first time. It was jealousy that was the basis of it — the emotion which survives every other passion of mankind, Peter Walsh thought, holding his pocket-knife at arm's length. Daisy had told him in her last letter that she was meeting Major Orde; just to make him jealous, he knew. He was furious! All this business of coming to England to see lawyers was not to marry her, but to stop her from marrying someone else. That was what tortured him when he saw Clarissa so calm, so cold, and realised what she had made him into: a tearful old fool!

Mr and Mrs Septimus Warren Smith crossed the road. They were going to Sir William Bradshaw; she thought his name sounded nice; he would cure Septimus at once. It was a silly dream, being unhappy. Did anyone suspect that here is a young man who is the happiest man in the world, and the most miserable? Perhaps they walked more slowly than other people, and there was something hesitating[1] in the man's walk, but what is more natural for a clerk, who has not been in the West End on a weekday at this hour for years, than to keep looking at the sky. To look at him, he might have been a better-looking clerk; he wore brown boots; his hands were educated; his profile was educated, sensitive. He was a border case, neither one thing nor the other, who might eventually have a house and a motor car or continue renting apartments in back streets all his life; a half-educated, self-educated man whose education is all learnt from books

---

1. hesitating: 猶疑不定

borrowed from public libraries, read in the evening after the day's work.

London has swallowed up[1] many millions of young men called Smith and has thought nothing of fantastic Christian names like Septimus. Renting a room off the Euston Road, there were experiences which in two years changed an innocent face into a lean[2] and hostile[3] one. Shy and stammering[4], Septimus was anxious to improve himself. When he fell in love with Miss Isabel Pole, lecturing in the Waterloo Road upon Shakespeare, lighting in him the kind of fire that burns only once in a lifetime, his employer Mr Brewer knew that something was up[5]. Septimus's managing clerk thought very highly of Smith's abilities, predicting great things for him 'if he keeps his health', for Smith looked weakly. Mr Brewer advised football, invited him to supper and was in the process of recommending a rise in Smith's salary, when something happened which interfered with his calculations and took away his ablest[6] young men: the European War.

Septimus was one of the first to volunteer. He went to France and instantly developed what Mr Brewer had intended from football: manliness. He was promoted; he drew the attention, indeed the affection of his officer, Evans. They shared everything — the fighting, the personal quarrels. But when Evans — a 'quiet man', according to Rezia, who had only seen him once — was killed in Italy in 1918, Septimus showed hardly any emotion and congratulated himself upon feeling very little. The War had taught him. He had seen everything: friendship, war, death, promotion, and he was still under thirty. He was bound to survive. When peace came he was in Milan,

---

1. **swallowed up:** 榨取
2. **lean:** 瘦削
3. **hostile:** 兇狠
4. **stammering:** 結巴
5. **something was up:** 有事不妥
6. **ablest:** 健壯

living in the house of an innkeeper with two daughters who made hats; and one evening, panicking about his inability to feel, he became engaged to Lucrezia, the younger daughter; the gay[1], frivolous[2] one. 'It is the hat that matters most,' she would say, when they walked out together. 'Beautiful!' she would murmur, nudging[3] Septimus, that he might see.

'The English are so silent,' Rezia said. She liked it, she said. She respected these Englishmen, and wanted to see London.

At the office he was given a post of considerable responsibility. They were proud of him; he had won crosses[4]. 'You have done your duty; it is up to us —' began Mr Brewer; and could not finish, so pleasurable was his emotion. They took admirable lodgings[5] off the Tottenham Court Road. He opened Shakespeare again and realised that the intoxication[6] of language had deserted him. The secret message hidden in the beauty of words was hatred and despair. Meanwhile Rezia sat at the table trimming hats. She looked pale, mysterious, like a lily, drowned, under water, he thought.

'The English are so serious,' she would say, putting her arms round Septimus, her cheek against his. Rezia said, she must have children. They had been married five years. She must have a boy, a son like Septimus, she said. SHE could not grow old and have no children! She was very lonely, she was very unhappy! She cried for the first time since they were married. But he felt nothing.

At last, with a melodramatic gesture, mechanical, insincere, he dropped his head on his hands. Now he had surrendered; now other people must help him. People must be sent for. He gave in.

Nothing could rouse him. Rezia put him to bed. She sent for a

---

1. **gay:** 高興
2. **frivolous:** 輕佻
3. **nudging:** 用肘輕推

4. **crosses:** 表揚軍功的十字勳章
5. **lodgings:** 住宿
6. **intoxication:** 吸引力

doctor. There was nothing whatever the matter, said Dr Holmes. Oh, what a relief! What a kind man, what a good man! thought Rezia. So there was no excuse; nothing the matter at all, except the sin of not feeling: not caring when Evans was killed; seducing and marrying his wife without loving her. The verdict of human nature on such a bad person was death.

Dr Holmes came again. He dismissed[1] everything — the headaches, sleeplessness, fears, dreams — it was nerve symptoms and nothing more, he said. Throw yourself into outside interests; take up some hobby, said Dr Holmes, for did he not owe his own excellent health (and he worked as hard as any man in London) to the fact that he could always switch off[2]?

When the damned fool came again, Septimus refused to see him. Dr Holmes smiled, pushed past Mrs Smith in a friendly way and sat down beside his patient. Wouldn't it be better to do something instead of lying in bed? Forty years of experience told him that there was nothing the matter at all with him. Dr Holmes came quite regularly every day. Rezia could not understand him. Dr Holmes was such a kind man. He was so interested in Septimus. He only wanted to help them, he said.

So he was deserted. The world was shouting: kill yourself, kill yourself, but he was too weak. Holmes had won of course. At that moment Rezia came in from shopping, with her flowers, and walked across the room, and put the roses in a vase, upon which the sun struck directly.

'Communication is health; communication is happiness,' he muttered.

---

1. **dismissed:** 不屑一顧
2. **switch off:** 放鬆

'What are you saying, Septimus?' Rezia asked, wild with terror, for he was talking to himself.

She sent for Dr Holmes. Her husband, she said, was mad. He hardly knew her.

'You brute[1]! You brute!' cried Septimus, seeing human nature, in the form of Dr Holmes, enter the room.

'Now what's all this about?' said Dr Holmes in the most amiable[2] way in the world. 'Talking nonsense to frighten your wife?' But he would give him something to make him sleep. And if they were rich people, said Dr Holmes, looking ironically round the room, of course they could go to Harley Street[3]; if they had no confidence in him, said Dr Holmes, looking not quite so kind.

---

1. **brute:** 畜生
2. **amiable:** 和藹可親的
3. **Harley Street:** 哈雷街，倫敦名醫集中地

Grammar

1 **Use these key words to make complete sentences. Think carefully about the verbs — and you might have to add a word or two!**

   1 Milan / decide / (not) suffer / any / go back / Lucrezia / so / would / more / that

   2 Peter / differently / away / five / how / India / after / people / notice / behave / years

   3 Seton / the / ! / nobody / kiss / Hugh / penniless / that / Sally / Whitbread / believe / smoking-room

   4 Septimus / football / take up / work / Mr / stay / Brewer / want / by / healthy

   5 silent / Italy / so / they / like / English / Rezia / because / be

   6 ill / Dr / accept / say / matter / Holmes / refuse / that / be / Septimus / nothing / there / be

Making Sense — Use your own words

2 **Look at these examples from Chapter Four. Rewrite them, using your own words and making sure that the meaning is unchanged.**

   1 She could stand it no longer.

   2 She detested him for some reason; she had something against him.

   3 They could never survive on less than five hundred pounds a year.

   4 She had that extraordinary gift of making a world of her own.

   5 That was what tortured him when he saw Clarissa so calm, so cold...

   6 Septimus was anxious to improve himself.

   7 He was one of the first to volunteer.

   8 The verdict of human nature on such a bad person was death.

Reading Comprehension

3 Make notes about Septimus and Rezia's marriage in the chart below and then compare it with Clarissa and Richard Dalloway's.

THE WARREN SMITHS' MARRIAGE	THE DALLOWAYS' MARRIAGE

Speaking

4 What does Septimus mean when he says "Communication is health; communication is happiness". How does this remark connect to the characters which you have read about so far in this book?

Text Analysis

5 Can you identify who is speaking and what the situation is?

1 'My hand has grown so thin.'

_____

2 'You represent all that is most detestable in British middle-class life!'

_____

3 'It's only that, after seeing her, I keep thinking about her.'

_____

4 'You look pale, mysterious, like a lily, drowned, under water.'

_____

5 'You should think about taking up a hobby and having outside interests.'

_____

6 'You brute!'

_____

Reading Comprehension

6 **Are these statements true (T) or false (F)?**

		T	F
1	Septimus feels guilty about not being affected by the death of his friend Evans.	☐	☐
2	Peter thinks that Sally Seton is the best of Clarissa's friends.	☐	☐
3	Mrs Hugh is a wild, daring, romantic woman.	☐	☐
4	Peter is quite a lot older that Hugh.	☐	☐
5	Peter is no longer in love with Clarissa.	☐	☐
6	When Septimus came back from the War, he was given an important job at his company.	☐	☐
7	After the War, Septimus was no longer interested in the language of Shakespeare.	☐	☐
8	Septimus is always pleased to see Dr Holmes.	☐	☐

Grammar

7 **Look at these extracts from the chapter. Re-write them in indirect speech, using the verb in CAPITALS.**

"Communication is happiness," he muttered. DECIDE
He decided that communication was happiness.

1 Lucrezia Warren Smith was saying to herself, It's wicked. THINK

_____

2 'I have put the ring in my purse,' she told him. INFORM

_____

3 He thinks of nothing but his own appearance, she said. COMMENT

_____

4 'It is the hat that matters most,' she would say. BE CONVINCED

_____

5 'You have done your duty; it is up to us —' began Mr Brewer. INSIST

_____

Writing

8 In Chapter Five Septimus and Rezia visit an important medical expert in an exclusive part of London. What do you think the doctor will say to Septimus? Write your ideas.

_____

_____

_____

_____

_____

_____

Vocabulary

9 The following words appear in Chapter Five. Write their synonyms.

1 send away_____

2 an appropriate balance _____

3 tiredness_____

4 abandoned_____

5 cry with great emotion_____

6 a warm covering for the body_____

Speaking

10 Look at the picture on page 69. The doctor, Sir William Bradshaw, is speaking to Reiza. What kind of person do you think he is?

_____

_____

_____

Chapter Five

A Sense of Proportion

▶ 4 It was precisely twelve o'clock by Big Ben as Clarissa Dalloway laid her green dress on her bed, and the Warren Smiths walked down Harley Street. Twelve was the hour of their appointment. Probably, Rezia thought, that was Sir William Bradshaw's house with the grey motor car in front of it.

Yes, it was Sir William Bradshaw's motor car; low, powerful, grey; and to match its sober[1] nature, there were silver grey rugs inside, to keep her ladyship warm while she waited. For often Sir William would travel sixty miles or more down into the country to visit the rich, the afflicted[2], who could afford the very large fee which Sir William very properly charged for his advice. Her ladyship waited with the rugs around her knees for an hour or more, leaning back, thinking sometimes of the patient, sometimes, understandably, of the increasing money, as she waited minute by minute; the 'wall of gold' which would distance them from their anxieties (they had had their struggles) until she felt as if she were floating on a calm ocean; respected, admired, with almost nothing left to wish for, though she regretted her size; large dinner-parties every Thursday night to the profession; too little time, unfortunately, with her husband, whose work increased; a son doing well at Eton[3]; she would have

1. **sober:** 素淡
2. **afflicted:** 患病的

3. **Eton:** 伊頓公學，英國著名男校

liked a daughter too. She had plenty of interests: child welfare; the after-care of the epileptic, and photography, so that, while she waited, if there was a church building, or a church in disrepair, she managed to get the key and take photographs, which were almost professional in quality, hardly to be distinguished from the work of professionals.

Sir William himself was no longer young. He had worked very hard; he had won his position by sheer ability (being the son of a shopkeeper); he loved his profession. He looked impressive at ceremonies and spoke well — and, by the time he became 'Sir' William, all these things had given him a heavy, weary look (the stream of patients being so incessant[1], the responsibilities and privileges of his profession so onerous[2]). This weariness, together with his grey hair, increased the extraordinary distinction of his presence and gave him the reputation (very important when dealing with nerve cases) not only of lightning skill[3], and almost infallible[4] accuracy in diagnosis but of sympathy; tact; understanding of the human soul. He could see the first moment they came into the room (the Warren Smiths they were called); he was certain as soon as he saw the man; it was a case of extreme gravity[5]. It was a case of complete physical and nervous breakdown, with every symptom in an advanced stage, he discovered in two or three minutes (writing answers to questions, asked quietly and discreetly, on a pink card).

How long had Dr Holmes been attending him?

Six weeks.

Had he prescribed a little bromide? Had he said there was nothing the matter? Ah yes (those general practitioners[6]! thought

1. **incessant:** 持續不斷
2. **onerous:** 沉重
3. **lightning skill:** 快而準的診療技巧
4. **infallible:** 極少出錯的
5. **gravity:** 嚴重
6. **practitioners:** 私人執業醫生

Sir William. It took half his time to make good their mistakes. Some were irreparable).

'You served with great distinction in the War?'

The patient repeated the word 'war' questioningly.

He was attaching meanings to words of a symbolical kind. A serious symptom, to be noted on the card.

'The War?' the patient asked. The European War — that little game for schoolboys with explosives? Had he served with distinction? He really forgot. In the War itself he had failed.

'Yes, he served with the greatest distinction,' Rezia assured the doctor; 'he was promoted.'

'And they have the very highest opinion of you at your office?' Sir William murmured, glancing at Mr Brewer's very generously worded letter. 'So that you have nothing to worry you, no financial anxiety, nothing?'

He had committed an appalling[1] crime and been condemned to death by human nature.

'I have — I have,' he began, 'committed a crime —'

'He has done nothing wrong whatever,' Rezia assured the doctor. If Mr Smith would wait, said Sir William, he would speak to Mrs Smith in the next room. Her husband was very seriously ill, Sir William said. Did he threaten to kill himself?

Oh, he did, she cried. But he did not mean it, she said. Of course not. It was simply a question of rest, said Sir William; of rest, rest, rest; a long rest in bed. There was a delightful rest home down in the country where her husband would be perfectly looked after. Away from her? she asked. Unfortunately, yes; the people we care for most are not good

1. **appalling:** 令人髮指

for us when we are ill. But he was not mad, was he? Sir William said he never spoke of 'madness'; he called it not having a sense of proportion. But her husband did not like doctors. He would refuse to go there. Shortly and kindly Sir William explained to her the state of the case. He had threatened to kill himself. There was no alternative. It was a question of law. He would lie in bed in a beautiful house in the country. The nurses were admirable. Sir William would visit him once a week. If Mrs Warren Smith was quite sure she had no more questions to ask — he never hurried his patients — they would return to her husband. She had nothing more to ask — not of Sir William.

So they returned to the 'criminal'; the victim exposed; the fugitive[1]; to Septimus Warren Smith, who sat in the arm-chair under the skylight staring at a photograph of Lady Bradshaw, muttering messages about beauty.

'We have had our little talk,' said Sir William.

'He says you are very, very ill,' Rezia cried.

'We have been arranging that you should go into a home,' said Sir William.

'One of Holmes's homes?' asked Septimus dismissively[2].

This man made a distasteful impression. For there was in Sir William, whose father had been a tradesman, a natural respect for breeding[3] and clothing. There was in Sir William, who had never had time for reading, a deep prejudice against cultivated people who came into his room and intimated that doctors, whose profession challenges all the highest faculties[4], are not educated men.

'One of MY homes, Mr Warren Smith,' he said, 'where we will teach you to rest.'

---

1. **fugitive:** 犯人
2. **dismissively:** 輕蔑地
3. **breeding:** 教養

4. **challenges...faculties:** 指醫生的心志 往往受到最嚴格的考驗

And there was just one more thing.

He was quite certain that when Mr Warren Smith was well he was the last man in the world to frighten his wife. But he had talked of killing himself.

'We all have our moments of depression,' said Sir William.

Once you fall, Septimus repeated to himself, human nature attacks you. Holmes and Bradshaw attack you. Human nature shows no pity.

'Impulses came upon him sometimes?' Sir William asked, with his pencil on a pink card.

That was his own business[1], said Septimus.

'Nobody lives for himself alone,' said Sir William, glancing at the photograph of his wife.

'And you have a brilliant career before you,' said Sir William. There was Mr Brewer's letter on the table. 'An exceptionally brilliant career.'

But if he confessed? If he communicated? Would his torturers let him go?

'I— I—' he stammered.

But what was his crime? He could not remember it.

'Yes?' Sir William encouraged him. (But it was growing late.)

Love, trees, there is no crime — what was his message?

He could not remember it.

'I— I—' Septimus stammered.

'Try to think as little about yourself as possible,' said Sir William kindly. Really, in his condition, this man should not be out and about[2].

Was there anything else they wished to ask him? Sir William would make all arrangements (he murmured to Rezia) and he would let her know between five and six that evening, he murmured.

---

1. **business:** 私事
2. **out and about:** 到處閒逛

'Trust everything to me,' he said, and then he dismissed them.

Never, never had Rezia felt such agony in her life! She had asked for help and been deserted! He had failed them! Sir William Bradshaw was not a nice man.

Simply maintaining that motor car must cost him quite a lot, said Septimus, when they got out into the street.

She held his arm tightly. They had been deserted.

But what more did she want?

To his patients Sir William Bradshaw gave three-quarters of an hour; and if in this exacting[1] science which has to do with what we actually know nothing about — the nervous system, the human brain — a doctor loses his sense of proportion, as a doctor he fails. Health is something we must have; and health is proportion; so that when a man comes into your room with a message (like most patients), and threatens, as they often do, to kill himself, you invoke[2] proportion; order rest in bed; rest in solitude; silence and rest; rest without friends, without books, without messages; six months' rest; until a man who went in weighing seven stone six comes out weighing twelve.

Proportion, divine proportion, Sir William's goddess, was acquired by Sir William walking hospitals, catching salmon, having one son in Harley Street by Lady Bradshaw, who caught salmon herself and took photographs almost on the level of a professional. Worshipping proportion, Sir William not only prospered[3] himself but made England prosper, secluded her lunatics[4], forbade childbirth, penalised[5] despair, made it impossible for the unfit to propagate[6] their views until they, too, shared his sense of proportion — his, if they were men, Lady Bradshaw's if they were women (she embroidered,

---

1. **exacting:** 嚴謹的
2. **invoke:** 喚起
3. **prospered:** 成功
4. **secluded her lunatics:** 使她的精神病人與世隔絕
5. **penalised:** 懲治
6. **propagate:** 宣揚

knitted, spent four nights out of seven at home with her son), so that not only did his colleagues respect him, his subordinates[1] fear him, but the friends and relations of his patients felt for him the keenest[2] gratitude for insisting that those patients who predicted the end of the world should drink milk in bed, as Sir William ordered; Sir William with his thirty years' experience of these kinds of cases, and his infallible instinct, this is madness, this is sense; in fact, his sense of proportion.

But there is another side to this Proportion — less smiling, more formidable — in the heat of India, the mud of Africa, the outer regions of London, wherever the climate or the devil tempts men to abandon true belief for Conversion. It can be seen taking advantage of the weak; seen in those people wanting to impress and to impose. At Hyde Park Corner[3] it is in the preaching[4], standing on a tub; it is disguised as brotherly love through factories and parliaments; it offers help, but desires power; it dismisses those who do not feel, those who are dissatisfied. Rezia Warren Smith guessed that conversion was in Sir William's heart, although hidden under the name of love, duty, self-sacrifice. How he would work hard to raise money, propagate reforms, initiate institutions! But conversion loves blood better than buildings and brick, and eats away at the human will. Take, for example, Lady Bradshaw. Fifteen years ago she had gone under[5]. It was nothing you could put your finger on; there had been no scene, no snap; only the slow sinking of her will into his. Her smile was sweet, her submission was rapid; an eight- or nine-course dinner in Harley Street, feeding ten or fifteen professional guests, was smooth and relaxed. Only as the evening continued, there was a very slight

---

1. **subordinates:** 下屬
2. **keenest:** 最強烈的
3. **Hyde Park Corner:** 倫敦海德公園的著名演講空地
4. **preaching:** 佈道
5. **had gone under:** 這裏指被打敗

uneasiness perhaps, nervousness and confusion indicated, what it was really painful to believe — that the poor lady lied. Once, long ago, she had caught salmon freely: now, wanting to satisfy her husband's eye for power, she drew back; so that, without knowing precisely what made the evening disagreeable, and caused this pressure on the top of the head (was it the professional conversation, or the fatigue of a great doctor whose life, Lady Bradshaw said, 'is not his own but his patients'?), it *was* disagreeable: so that guests, when the clock struck ten, breathed in the air of Harley Street with excitement; which relief, however, was denied to his patients.

There in Sir William's grey room, with the pictures on the wall, and the valuable furniture, they learnt the extent of their transgressions[1]; huddled up[2] in arm-chairs, they watched him go through, for their benefit, a curious exercise with the arms, which he shot out[3], brought sharply back to his hip, to prove (if the patient was obstinate)[4] that Sir William was master of his own actions, which the patient was not. Some patients broke down weakly; sobbed, submitted; others, inspired by Heaven knows what intemperate[5] madness, called Sir William insincere to his face; even more disrespectfully, questioned life itself. Why live? they demanded. Sir William replied that life was good. Certainly Lady Bradshaw's portrait hung over the mantelpiece, and as for his income it was quite twelve thousand a year. But to us, they protested, life has given no such abundance.[6] He agreed. They lacked a sense of proportion. And perhaps, after all, there is no God? He shrugged his shoulders. In short, this living or not living is

1. **transgressions:** 犯規
2. **huddled up:** 蜷縮
3. **shot out:** 射出、快速地伸出

4. **obstinate:** 冥頑不靈
5. **intemperate:** 過度
6. **abundance:** 這裏指美好的經歷

an affair of our own[1]? But there they were mistaken. Sir William had a friend in Surrey where they taught, what Sir William frankly admitted was a difficult art — a sense of proportion. There was, moreover, family affection; honour; courage; and a brilliant career. All of these had in Sir William a resolute champion. Defenceless, the exhausted, the friendless received the full impact of Sir William's will. He attacked and he destroyed. He shut people up. It was this combination of decision and humanity that made Sir William so popular with the relations of his victims.

But Rezia Warren Smith cried, walking down Harley Street, which advised submission, upheld[2] authority, and pointed out in chorus the supreme advantages of a sense of proportion, that she did not like that man.

A commercial clock, suspended above a shop in Oxford Street, announced, genially[3] and fraternally[4], that it was half-past one.

---

1. **an affair of our own:** 關乎人類的事
2. **upheld:** 支持
3. **genially:** 和藹地；歡快地
4. **fraternally:** 像兄弟一般；充滿友愛地

Text Analysis

1 Can you identify who is speaking and what the situation is?

1 'You served with great distinction in the War?'

_____

2 'I have — I have ... committed a crime —'

_____

3 'Away from me?'

_____

4 'Simply maintaining that motor car must cost him quite a lot'.

_____

5 'His life is not his own but his patients'.

_____

6 'I do not like that man!'

_____

Sentence-building

2 Use these key words to make complete sentences. Think carefully about the verbs — and you might have to add a word or two!

1 case / Warren Smiths / gravity / Sir / this / see / the / be / When / a / come into / room / extreme / his / William Bradshaw / that

2 death / Septimus / condemn / nature / feel / human / that / him

3 husband / Sir William / stay away / her / have to / tell / Rezia / would / that / she

4 be abandoned / Rezia / she / Sir William / feel / Septimus / and / that

5 Sir William / experience / of / doctor / a / sense / thirty / proportion / years / have / a / of / with

6 Bradshaw / ago / sacrifice (_verb_) / Lady / will (_noun_) / Fifteen / sake / husband's / the / years / ambition / her / her

Reading Comprehension

3 **Are these statements true (T) or false (F)?**

		T	F
1	The Warren Smiths have an appointment at 11 o'clock.	☐	☐
2	Septimus is a case of complete physical and nervous breakdown.	☐	☐
3	Sir William has a deep prejudice against people like Rezia from Italy.	☐	☐
4	We actually know nothing about the nervous system and the human brain.	☐	☐
5	There are two sides to Proportion.	☐	☐
6	Lady Bradshaw has never been fishing in her life.	☐	☐
7	Patients feel a deep sincerity in Sir William.	☐	☐
8	Septimus told Rezia that he did not like Sir William.	☐	☐

Grammar

4 **Look at these extracts from the chapter. Re-write them in indirect speech, using the verb in CAPITALS.**

'He says you are very, very ill,' Rezia cried. BE AFRAID
Rezia was afraid that he was very ill.

1 'You served with great distinction in the War?' Sir William asked. INQUIRE

_____

2 Rezia assured the doctor, 'He was promoted.' TELL

_____

3 Septimus did not mean to kill himself, Rezia said. INSIST

_____

4 'We will teach you to rest, Mr Warren Smith,' said Sir William. INFORM

_____

5 'And you have a brilliant career before you,' said Sir William. ASSURE

_____

Reading Comprehension

5 **Look at these sentences from the chapter you have just read. Can you put them into context and explain their meaning?**

1 'The 'wall of gold' which would distance them from their anxieties...'

_____

2 'This weariness ... increased the extraordinary distinction of his presence.'

_____

3 'He was attaching meanings to words of a symbolical kind.'

_____

4 'He never hurried his patients'

_____

5 'It was nothing you could put your finger on.'

_____

6 'Which relief, however, was denied to his patients.'

_____

Grammar

6 **Here is a summary of Chapter Five, but some of the facts and the verbs are wrong! Correct them.**

Septimus and Rezia was walking up Bond Street for a twelve o'clock appointment with Sir William Bradshaw. They see a black motor-car outside his house. When Sir William was first seeing Septimus, he did not think it is a serious case. Septimus tells him that he had been seeing Dr Holmes for two months. Sir William tells Rezia in front of her husband that Septimus would have needed plenty of rest in one of his homes in the city. She would be able to visit him once a week. Septimus is very happy at this suggestion and Sir William says that he will make all the arrangements. Rezia and Septimus leave and she decided that she was liking Sir William a lot. It is a quarter past one when they are in Oxford Street.

Grammar

7a **These adjectives appear in Chapter Six. Write the noun next to each one.**

1 magnificent _____
2 unsuccessful _____
3 memorable _____
4 poor _____
5 contemplative _____
6 silent _____

7b **Now do the same as 7a, except that now you have to write the adverbs next to these nouns from Chapter Six.**

1 affection _____
2 deception _____
3 miracle _____
4 happiness _____
5 person _____

7c **Now write five sentences of your own, using the adverbs above.**

1 _____
2 _____
3 _____
4 _____
5 _____

8 **This chapter is called *Lunching with a Lady* and it involves Richard Dalloway and Hugh Whitbread. Write down some ideas about what the topic(s) of conversation will be.**

_____
_____
_____
_____

Chapter Six

Lunching with a Lady

Hugh Whitbread hesitated in front of the window of that same shop in Oxford Street; it was his habit. He was not a deep person; once upon a time the topics of conversation were the dead languages and the living ones; life in Constantinople, Paris, Rome; riding, shooting, tennis. Unkind people would say that he now kept guard[1] at Buckingham Palace — guarding what, nobody knew. But he did it extremely efficiently. He had known Prime Ministers. His affections were understood to be deep.

As he paused to consider the socks and shoes in the shop window, Hugh looked magnificent: impeccable, and dressed to match. Then he remembered the old-fashioned ceremonies which gave a memorable quality to his manner: he would never lunch, for example, with Lady Bruton, whom he had known for the past twenty years, without bringing her a bunch of carnations and asking Miss Brush, Lady Bruton's secretary, how her brother in South Africa was. For some reason, Miss Brush, though she was completely charmless[2], resented Hugh's question so much that she said 'Thank you, he's doing very well in South Africa,' when, for half a dozen years, he had been doing badly in Portsmouth.

Lady Bruton herself preferred Richard Dalloway, who arrived at

1. **kept guard:** 守衛
2. **charmless:** 毫無吸引力

the next moment. (Indeed he and Hugh met on the doorstep.) Richard Dalloway was made of much finer material[1]. But she wouldn't let anyone talk badly of her poor dear Hugh. She could never forget his remarkable kindness. At the age of sixty-two, Lady Bruton did not cut people up — as Clarissa Dalloway did — and stick them together again.

She took Hugh's carnations unsmilingly. There was nobody else for lunch, she said, she had tricked them into coming[2], to help her out of a difficulty —

'But let us eat first,' she said.

And so there began a silent moving through swing doors of housemaids in aprons and white caps, as part of a grand deception practised by hostesses in Mayfair[3] from one-thirty to two o'clock, when the traffic stops and on the table is glass and silver, fruit and casseroles of chicken. The fire burns; and the wine and the coffee bring joyful visions to contemplative eyes. Life appears musical, mysterious.

Those eyes now saw the beauty of the red carnations which Lady Bruton had put beside her plate, so that Hugh Whitbread, feeling at peace with the entire universe, said:

'Wouldn't they look charming against your lace[4]?'

Miss Brush disliked this familiarity intensely. She thought he was uncultured.

Lady Bruton held up the carnations, rather stiffly. Then she thought: I had better wait until they have had their coffee to ask the favour; and so she put them down again beside her plate.

'How's Clarissa?' she asked abruptly. Clarissa always said that Lady Bruton did not like her.

1. **made of much finer material:** 比……優秀得多
2. **tricked them into coming:** 指邀請客人來是另有原因
3. **Mayfair:** 倫敦市中心的高尚地段
4. **against your lace:** 戴在花邊衣服上

'I met Clarissa in the Park this morning,' said Hugh Whitbread, helping himself enthusiastically to the casserole. One of the greediest[1] men she had ever known, Milly Brush thought.

'D'you know who's in town?' said Lady Bruton suddenly. 'Our old friend, Peter Walsh.'

They all smiled. Peter Walsh! And Mr Dalloway was genuinely glad, Milly Brush thought; and Mr Whitbread thought only of his chicken.

Peter Walsh! All three, Lady Bruton, Hugh Whitbread, and Richard Dalloway, remembered the same thing — how passionately Peter had been in love; been rejected; gone to India; got into trouble. Richard Dalloway was very fond of Peter, Milly Brush saw that. She saw him hesitate; consider; this interested her, just as Mr Dalloway always interested her; what was he thinking, she wondered, about Peter Walsh?

That Peter Walsh had been in love with Clarissa; that he would go back directly after lunch and find Clarissa; that he would tell her that he loved her.

'Yes; Peter Walsh has come back,' she said, 'exhausted, unsuccessful.' But to help him, they reflected, was impossible; there was some flaw[2] in his character. Hugh Whitbread said he might of course mention his name to somebody — he thought solemnly of the letters he would write to the heads of Government offices about 'my old friend, Peter Walsh.' But it wouldn't result in anything permanent, because of his character.

'In trouble with some woman,' said Lady Bruton. They had all guessed that THAT was the reason.

1. **greediest:** 指貪吃太多而顯得無禮
2. **flaw:** 瑕疵

'However,' said Lady Bruton, anxious to leave the subject, 'we shall hear the whole story from Peter himself.'

Lady Bruton was getting impatient; she was concentrating on that subject which engaged the attention, the soul of Millicent Bruton; that project for emigrating young people of both sexes born of respectable parents and setting them up[1] with a reasonable prospect of doing well in Canada. But she had to write a letter to the Times[2]. After a morning's battle beginning, tearing up, beginning again, she now turned to Hugh Whitbread, who famously possessed the art of writing letters to the Times.

So she let Hugh eat his soufflé; and she asked after poor Evelyn. She waited until they were smoking, and then said:

'Milly, would you fetch the papers?'

Miss Brush went out, came back; laid papers on the table; and Hugh produced his silver fountain pen, which had done twenty years' service, he said. He marvellously reduced Lady Bruton's confusions to sense and to grammar. Lady Bruton watched the transformation. Hugh was slow but persistent; Richard said one must take risks and laughed at Hugh's deference[3] to people's feelings. Finally, Hugh read out the draft[4] of a letter which Lady Bruton felt certain was a masterpiece. He could not guarantee that the editor would put it in; but he would be meeting somebody at lunch.

On hearing this, Lady Bruton stuffed all Hugh's carnations into the front of her dress, and throwing her hands out called him 'My Prime Minister!' The two men got up. As they stood in the hall taking their gloves from the bowl on the table, Hugh politely offered Miss Brush a ticket to some event, which she hated from the depths of her

---

1. **setting them up:** 幫他們辦理手續
2. **Times:** 泰晤士報，英國報章
3. **deference:** 禮讓
4. **draft:** 草稿

heart and which made her blush[1]. Richard turned to Lady Bruton, with his hat in his hand, and said:

'We shall see you at our party tonight?'

Lady Bruton said she might come; or she might not come. Clarissa had wonderful energy. Parties terrified Lady Bruton. But then, she was getting old…

Lady Bruton went majestically up to her room and lay down. Those kind good fellows, Richard Dalloway, Hugh Whitbread, had gone this hot day through the streets whose sounds came up to her lying on the sofa. And the two men went further and further from her, being attached to her by a thin thread[2] (since they had lunched with her) which would stretch and stretch[3], get thinner and thinner as they walked across London.

Lady Bruton slept. And Richard Dalloway and Hugh Whitbread hesitated at the corner of Conduit Street at the exact moment that Millicent Bruton, lying on the sofa, let the thread break; she snored. They looked in at a shop window; they did not wish to buy or to talk but to say goodbye. However, they paused. The speed of the morning traffic diminished.

Richard could not think or move. Hugh Whitbread was admiring a Spanish necklace which he thought Evelyn might like. Richard yawned. Hugh was going into the shop.

'All right!' said Richard, following.

He really didn't want to go buying necklaces with Hugh. He never gave Clarissa presents, except a bracelet[4] two or three years ago, which had not been a success. She never wore it. Richard's mind, recovering from its lethargy[5], focused now on his wife, Clarissa, whom Peter

1. **blush:** 臉紅
2. **thread:** 線，這裏作比喻用
3. **stretch and stretch:** 不斷延伸
4. **bracelet:** 手鐲
5. **lethargy:** 死氣沉沉

Walsh had loved so passionately; and Richard suddenly saw their life together. He wanted to open the drawing-room door and come in holding a present for Clarissa. But what?

Flowers? Yes, any number of flowers, roses, orchids, to celebrate what was an event; this feeling about her when they spoke of Peter Walsh at lunch. They never spoke of it; they hadn't spoken of it for years; which, he thought, holding his large bunch of red and white roses, is the greatest mistake in the world. He walked towards Westminster intending to say directly (whatever she might think of him), holding out his flowers, 'I love you.' Why not? It was a miracle that he had married Clarissa; his life had been a miracle, he thought. He had, once upon a time, been jealous of Peter Walsh and Clarissa. But she had often said to him that she had been right not to marry Peter; which, knowing Clarissa, was obviously true. And here he was, in the prime of life[1], walking to his house in Westminster to tell Clarissa that he loved her. Happiness is this, he thought. Big Ben was beginning to strike, first the warning, musical; then the hour, irrevocable[2]. Lunch parties waste the entire afternoon, he thought, approaching his door.

The sound of Big Ben flooded Clarissa's drawing-room, where she sat, very annoyed, at her writing-table. It was perfectly true that she had not asked Ellie Henderson to her party; but she had done it intentionally. Now Mrs Marsham wrote, 'she had told Ellie Henderson she would ask Clarissa — Ellie desperately wanted to come.' But why should she invite all the dull women in London to her parties? Why should Mrs Marsham interfere?

The house bell filled the room with its melancholy tone; then she

---

1. **in the prime of life:** 到達人生高峰
2. **irrevocable:** 不能挽回的

heard, distractingly, something scratching at the door. Who at this hour? Three o'clock already, good Heavens! The door handle turned and in came Richard, holding out flowers! What a surprise! (But he could not bring himself to say he loved her; not exactly that.)

How lovely, she said, taking his flowers. She understood without his speaking. She put them in vases on the mantelpiece. How lovely they looked! she said. And was the lunch amusing, she asked? Had Lady Bruton asked after her? Peter Walsh was back. Mrs Marsham had written. Must she ask Ellie Henderson? That woman Kilman was upstairs with Elizabeth.

'But let us sit down for five minutes,' said Richard.

It all looked so empty. All the chairs were against the wall. What had they been doing? Oh, it was for the party; no, he had not forgotten. Peter Walsh was back. Oh yes; she had received him[1]. He was going to get a divorce; and he was in love with some woman in India. And he hadn't changed at all.

'Hugh was at lunch,' said Richard. She had met him too! Well, he was becoming absolutely intolerable. Buying Evelyn necklaces; fatter than ever before.

And I thought: 'I might have married you,' she said, thinking of Peter sitting there, opening and shutting his pocket-knife. 'Just as he always was, you know.'

'They were talking about him at lunch,' said Richard. (But he could not tell her he loved her. He held her hand. Happiness is this, he thought.) They had been writing a letter to the Times for Millicent Bruton.

'And our dear Miss Kilman?' he asked.

---

1. received him: 接待了他

'Kilman arrived, in a mackintosh with an umbrella, just as we had finished lunch,' Clarissa said. 'Elizabeth turned pink. They shut themselves in her room. I suppose they're praying.'

Richard didn't like it; but these things pass, if you let them.

'But why should I ask all the dull women in London to my parties?' said Clarissa.

It was very strange how much Clarissa cared about her parties, Richard thought. He had no idea of how a room should look. However, he must go, he said, getting up. He stood for a moment as if he were about to say something; and she wondered what? Why? There were the roses.

'Some Committee?' she asked, as he opened the door.

And there is a dignity in people; a solitude; a great division, even between husband and wife; and one must respect that, thought Clarissa, watching him.

Richard returned with a pillow and a quilt[1]. 'An hour's complete rest after lunch,' he said. And he went.

He would always say, 'An hour's complete rest after lunch' because a doctor had ordered it once. It was part of his adorable, divine simplicity; which made him go and do things, while she and Peter Walsh wasted their time arguing. But since he had brought the pillows, she would lie down...

Why did she suddenly feel, for no reason, desperately unhappy? It was something that Peter had said, combined with some of her depression; and what Richard had said had added to it, but what had he said? There were his roses. Her parties! Yes — her parties! Both of them criticised her very unfairly, laughed at her, for her parties. That was it!

1. **quilt:** 被子

Well, how was she going to defend herself? They thought — or Peter thought, anyway — that she enjoyed imposing herself[1]; liked to have famous people around her; was simply a snob. Richard just thought it was imprudent[2] of her to like excitement when she knew it was bad for her heart. It was childish, he thought.

Both were quite wrong. What she liked was simply life. 'That's what I do it for,' she said, speaking aloud, to life.

If Peter said to her, 'What's the sense of your parties?' all she could say was (and nobody could be expected to understand): they're an offering; which sounded terribly vague. She could not imagine Peter or Richard taking the trouble to give a party for no reason at all.

Anyway, it was her gift. She had nothing else of any importance; could not think, write, even play the piano. The notion that one day should follow another; Wednesday, Thursday, Friday, Saturday; that one should wake up in the morning; see the sky; walk in the park; meet Hugh Whitbread; suddenly have Peter Walsh come in; then have these roses from Richard; it was enough. After that, how unbelievable death was!

And no one in the whole world would know how she had loved every instant…

1. **imposing herself:** 表現自己
2. **imprudent:** 輕率

Grammar

1 **Look at these examples from Chapter Six and re-write them in indirect speech, using the verb in CAPITALS.**

'Hugh was at lunch,' said Richard to Clarissa. INFORM
Richard informed Clarissa that Hugh had been at lunch.

1 'But let us sit down for five minutes,' said Richard. SUGGEST

2 'Do you know who's in town?' said Lady Bruton suddenly. ASK

3 'Yes, Peter Walsh has come back,' he said. CONFIRM

4 'However,' said Lady Bruton, 'we shall hear the whole story from Peter himself.' INSIST

5 'Kilman arrived, just as we had finished lunch,' Clarissa said to Elizabeth. TELL

Sentence-building

2 **Use these key words to make complete sentences. Think carefully about the verbs — and you might have to add a word or two!**

1 Dalloway / Although / flowers / Bruton / Richard / prefer / always / Hugh / bring / Lady

2 character / because / Hugh / be afraid / flaw / (not) be able to / job / Peter / for / he / a / in / his / find / permanent / a

3 masterpiece / After / call / finish / the *Times* / Bruton / Hugh / letter / enthusiastic / Lady / be / a / and

4 Clarissa / flowers / love / Richard / to give / bunch / want / tell / that / her / and / he

Making Sense of the Text

3 **Look at these sentences from Chapter Six. Explain their context, and their importance in the story, in your own words.**

1   His affections were understood to be deep.

_____

2   He had been doing badly in Portsmouth.

_____

3   Richard Dalloway was very fond of Peter.

_____

4   But it wouldn't result in anything permanent, because of his character.

_____

5   Hugh produced his silver fountain pen.

_____

6   The speed of the morning traffic diminished.

_____

7   Lunch parties waste the entire afternoon.

_____

8   But he could not bring himself to say he loved her.

_____

Vocabulary

4 **Look at these phrases and find their equivalent in the chapter.**

1   had not been very successful (in business)

_____

2   took out of his jacket

_____

3   liked (a lot)

_____

4   wearing appropriate clothes

_____

5   concluded

_____

6   as if he intended right now to...

_____

Text Analysis

5 Can you identify who is speaking?

1 'But let us eat first.'

_____

2 'I met Clarissa in the Park this morning.'

_____

3 'We shall see you at our party tonight?'

_____

4 'Why should I invite all the dull women in London to my parties?'

_____

5 'We've been writing a letter to the Times for Millicent Bruton.'

_____

6 'Some Committee?'

_____

Reading Comprehension

6 Are these statements true (T) or false (F)?

		T	F
1	Hugh Whitbread had always been a deep person, interested in dead languages.	☐	☐
2	Miss Brush dislikes Hugh Whitbread.	☐	☐
3	Clarissa likes to separate people and bring them together again.	☐	☐
4	Lady Bruton is surprised to hear that Peter Walsh is back in town.	☐	☐
5	Hugh and Richard are pleased to spend the afternoon together.	☐	☐
6	Clarissa is sitting in the drawing-room at her desk.	☐	☐
7	Richard and Peter would never give a party without a reason.	☐	☐

Vocabulary

7 Look at these words. The first is from the chapter you have just read; the other three are possible synonyms. Circle the one word which is NOT a synonym.

1	*intensely*	a lot	clearly	extremely
2	*impeccable*	imperfect	exemplary	perfect
3	*remarkable*	extraordinary	exceptional	exuberant
4	*desperately*	really	frustratedly	truly
5	*uncultured*	untrained	uneducated	ignorant
6	*genuinely*	seemingly	truly	sincerely

PRE-READING ACTIVITY

Reading Comprehension

8 Look at these phrases and write the equivalent in your own words.

1 She was quite **unaware** that she was being **observed**.

_____

2 She **found it intolerable** to see them together.

_____

3 People who **had the same** views as her...

_____

4 She **did not have enough money** to buy pretty clothes.

_____

5 She had almost **cried** suddenly...

_____

6 She had **been asked to leave**.

_____

Chapter Seven

A Singular Friendship

The door opened. Elizabeth knew that her mother was resting. She came in very quietly. She stood perfectly still. The Dalloways in general were fair-haired and blue-eyed; Elizabeth, however, was dark; had Chinese eyes in a pale face; an Oriental mystery; was gentle, considerate, still. As a child, she had had a perfect sense of humour; but now at seventeen (Clarissa could not understand why), she had become very serious; like a hyacinth[1] which has had no sun.

She stood quite still and looked at her mother; but the door was ajar[2], and outside was Miss Kilman, as Clarissa knew; Miss Kilman in her mackintosh, listening to whatever they said.

Miss Kilman had her reasons for wearing a mackintosh. First, it was cheap; second, she was over forty and she did not dress to please people. She was poor; otherwise she would not be working for the Dalloways (rich people who liked to be kind). In fact, Mr Dalloway had been kind, but Mrs Dalloway had not. She had been condescending[3]. They had expensive things everywhere; pictures, carpets, lots of servants. She considered that she had a perfect right to anything that the Dalloways did for her.

She had never been happy, being so clumsy[4] and so poor. The moment she had a chance at Miss Dolby's school, the War came.

1. hyacinth: 風信子
2. ajar: 微開的
3. condescending: 地位超然
4. clumsy: 笨手笨腳

Miss Dolby thought she would be happier with people who shared her views about the Germans. She had had to go. It was true that the family was of German origin; spelt the name Kiehlman in the eighteenth century; but her brother had been killed in the War. They sent her away because she would not pretend that the Germans were all villains. Mr Dalloway had found her working for the Friends[1]. He let her teach his daughter history. Then Our Lord had come to her — she had seen the light[2] two years and three months ago.

She did not envy women like Clarissa Dalloway; she pitied them. Instead of lying on a sofa — 'My mother is resting,' Elizabeth had said — she should have been in a factory; behind a counter; Mrs Dalloway and all the other fine ladies!

The Lord had shown her the way. So now, when she thought of her hatred of Mrs Dalloway, her grudge[3] against the world, she thought of God. Standing formidable in her mackintosh, she looked with steady and sinister serenity[4] at Mrs Dalloway, who came out with her daughter.

Elizabeth said she had forgotten her gloves. That was because Miss Kilman and her mother hated each other. She could not bear to see them together. She ran upstairs to find her gloves.

But Miss Kilman did not hate Mrs Dalloway. Observing Clarissa's small pink face, her delicate body, her air of freshness and fashion, Miss Kilman felt, fool! You have wasted your life, without knowing sorrow or pleasure! If only she could make her cry, You are right! But this was God's will, not Miss Kilman's. It was to be a religious victory. So she glared[5].

---

1. **the Friends:** 教友會，即 the Quakers 貴格會
2. **had seen the light:** 精神重生
3. **grudge:** 恨意

4. **with steady and sinister serenity:** 冷靜、嚴肅、神秘的神情
5. **glared:** 眼睛發亮

Clarissa was really shocked. This a Christian — this woman! This woman had taken her daughter from her! 'You are taking Elizabeth to the Stores[1]?' she said.

Miss Kilman said she was. They stood there. Miss Kilman was not going to be pleasant. And now Elizabeth arrived, rather out of breath, the beautiful girl.

As Miss Kilman stood there, like a prehistoric monster ready for battle, her hatred crumbled[2], her size diminished, and second by second she became Miss Kilman in a mackintosh, someone Clarissa would have liked to help!

As the monster got smaller and smaller, Clarissa laughed. Saying good-bye, she laughed.

Off they went together, Miss Kilman and Elizabeth, downstairs.

With a sudden impulse, for this woman was taking her daughter from her, Clarissa leant over the bannisters and cried out, 'Remember the party! Remember our party tonight!'

But Elizabeth had already opened the front door; there was a van passing; she did not answer.

Love and religion! thought Clarissa, going back into the drawing-room, how detestable they are! She watched out of the window the old lady opposite climbing upstairs. Let her climb upstairs if she wanted to; let her stop; then let her, as Clarissa had often seen her, reach her bedroom, part her curtains, and disappear again into the background. Somehow one respected that — that old woman looking out of the window, quite unconscious that she was being watched. It was a sight that made her want to cry.

Love destroyed everything that was fine. For example, with Peter

---

1. the Stores: 指 the Army and Navy Stores，專賣軍裝的服裝公司
2. crumbled: 崩潰

Walsh, here was a charming, clever man, with ideas about everything. Peter had helped her; Peter had lent her books. But look at the women he loved — vulgar, trivial, ordinary. He had come to see her after all these years, and what did he talk about? Himself!

Big Ben struck the half-hour.

It was extraordinary, strange, yes, touching[1], to see the old lady (they had been neighbours ever so many years) move away from the window, as if she were attached to the sound of Big Ben. She was forced, so Clarissa imagined, by that sound, to move, to go — but where? Clarissa tried to follow her as she turned and disappeared; she was moving at the back of the bedroom. She was still there moving about at the other end of the room. That old lady is the miracle, the supreme mystery, thought Clarissa: here was one room; there another. Did religion solve that, or love?

Clarissa Dalloway had insulted Miss Kilman; she had laughed at her for being ugly, clumsy, and not liking how she looked beside Mrs Dalloway. But Doris Kilman, standing still in the street, thought: why wish to resemble her? She despised[2] Mrs Dalloway from the bottom of her heart. But she had almost burst into tears when Clarissa Dalloway laughed at her. She could not help being ugly; she could not afford to buy pretty clothes. Anyhow, she had got Elizabeth. Sometimes lately it had seemed to her that, except for Elizabeth, her food was all that she lived for; her comforts; her dinner, her tea; her hot-water bottle at night.

Elizabeth had gone into the Army and Navy Stores — what department did she want? Elizabeth interrupted her thoughts.

'Petticoats[3],' she said abruptly, and walked to the lift. Elizabeth

1. touching: 感人
2. despised: 輕視
3. petticoats: 襯裙

guided her like a child. She chose one. While the serving girl packed it up, Elizabeth wondered what Miss Kilman was thinking. They must have their tea, said Miss Kilman.

Elizabeth thought Miss Kilman was hungry. She ate with intensity, then looked again and again at a plate of cakes on the table next to them. When a lady and a child sat down and the child took the cake, Miss Kilman was annoyed — the pleasure of eating was almost the only pure pleasure she had, and now not even that!

When people are happy, they have a reserve, she had told Elizabeth, upon which to draw. But she was like a wheel without a tyre (she was fond of such metaphors[1]). Miss Kilman had taken her to meetings, to a church in Kensington and for tea with a clergyman. She had lent her books. All professions are open to women of your generation, said Miss Kilman. But for herself, her career was absolutely ruined and was it her fault? Good heavens, of course not, said Elizabeth.

Mrs Dalloway sometimes called on Miss Kilman to bring her flowers — she was always very nice — but Miss Kilman squashed the flowers in a bunch, and she didn't have any social conversation or the same interests as Elizabeth's mother. Miss Kilman was extremely clever. Elizabeth had never thought about the poor, of course; her family lived with everything they wanted, her mother had breakfast in bed every day and she liked old women because they were Duchesses. But after one history lesson at the house, she had said, 'My grandfather kept an art shop in Kensington.' Miss Kilman made people feel so small.

Miss Kilman took another cup of tea. The oriental[2], mysterious Elizabeth sat perfectly upright; no, she did not want anything more.

1. **metaphors:** 隱喻
2. **oriental:** 東方的

She looked for her white gloves. They were under the table. Ah, but she must not go! Miss Kilman could not let her go! This beautiful girl, whom she genuinely loved!

Elizabeth would really like to go. But Miss Kilman said, 'I've not quite finished yet.'

Of course, then, Elizabeth would wait. But it was rather airless in here.

'Are you going to the party tonight?' Miss Kilman said. Elizabeth thought she would; her mother wanted her to go, even though she did not much like parties. Miss Kilman opened her mouth, finished her chocolate éclair[1], then wiped her fingers, and washed the tea round in her cup.

The agony was terrible, so terrific. If she could make Elizabeth her own, absolutely and forever, and then die; that was all she wanted. But to sit here, unable to think of anything to say; to see Elizabeth turning against her — it was too much; she could not stand it.

'I never go to parties,' said Miss Kilman, just to keep Elizabeth from going. 'People don't ask me to parties. Why should they ask me? I'm plain[2], I'm unhappy.' She knew it was idiotic. But she was Doris Kilman. She had her degree. Her knowledge of modern history was more than respectable.

'I don't pity myself,' she said. 'I pity'— she meant to say 'your mother' but no, she could not, not to Elizabeth. 'I pity other people,' she said, 'more.'

Elizabeth Dalloway sat silent. Was Miss Kilman going to say anything more?

'Don't quite forget me,' said Doris Kilman; her voice shook.

1. **éclair:** 法式指形小餅
2. **plain:** 其貌不揚

Elizabeth turned her head. The waitress came. Elizabeth went off to pay at the desk and then, turning and bowing her head very politely, she went.

She had gone. Miss Kilman sat at the marble table among the éclairs. Mrs Dalloway had triumphed[1]. Elizabeth had gone. Beauty had gone, youth had gone.

She got up, went off clumsily among the little tables; somebody came after her with her petticoat, and she lost her way. At last she came out into the street.

The tower of Westminster Cathedral rose in front of her, the habitation of God, in the midst of the traffic. She set off with her parcel, determined to get to that other sanctuary[2], Westminster Abbey. When she arrived there, she covered her face with her hands, like a tent. She seemed to struggle. Yet to others there, God was accessible and the path to Him was smooth. Having done their praying, they leant back, enjoyed the sweet music of the organ, and saw Miss Kilman at the end of the row, praying, praying, and thought of her sympathetically as a soul cut out of immaterial[3] substance; not a woman, a soul.

Elizabeth waited in Victoria Street for an omnibus. It was so nice to be out of doors. She thought perhaps she need not go home just yet. As she stood there, in her very well cut clothes, people were beginning to compare her to beauteous[4] nature, and it made her life difficult, for she much preferred being left alone to do what she liked in the country, but they would compare her to garden lilies, and she had to go to parties, and London was so boring compared with being alone in the country with her father and the dogs.

---

1. **triumphed:** 勝出
2. **sanctuary:** 聖殿

3. **immaterial:** 無形的
4. **beauteous:** 美麗

Her mother said she had such nice shoulders and held herself so straight, she was always charming to look at; and lately, in the evening especially, she looked almost beautiful, very serene. What could she be thinking? Every man fell in love with her, and she was really awfully bored. For it was beginning. Her mother could see that — the compliments were beginning. Clarissa sometimes worried that she did not care more about her clothes, for example; but it gave her a charm. And now there was this odd friendship with Miss Kilman. Well, thought Clarissa about three o'clock in the morning, reading because she could not sleep, it proves she has a heart.

Suddenly Elizabeth stepped forward and most competently boarded the omnibus, in front of everybody. She took a seat on top. And did Elizabeth give one thought to poor Miss Kilman, who loved her without jealousy? She was delighted to be free. The fresh air was so delicious. Miss Kilman was so difficult because she was always talking about her own sufferings.

She wanted to go a little further on the omnibus. Another penny was it to the Strand? Here was another penny then. She would go up the Strand.

She liked people who were ill. So she might be a doctor. She might be a farmer. Animals are often ill. She might own a thousand acres[1] and have people working for her. Somerset House[2] passed, a splendid, grey building. She liked the feeling of people working. It was so serious, so busy. In short, she would like to have a profession. She was quite determined to become either a farmer or a doctor — despite her mother. But she was, of course, rather lazy.

She must go home. She must dress for dinner. But what was the

1. **acres:** 英畝，約為 0.405 公頃
2. **Somerset House:** 薩默塞特府，位於倫敦市中心，曾是生死證明及婚姻註冊處

time? — where was a clock? She looked up Fleet Street. She walked just a little way towards St. Paul's, shyly; she did not dare wander off into strange alleys or tempting bye-streets[1]. No Dalloways came down the Strand daily; she was a pioneer, a wanderer, exploring and trusting.

In many ways, her mother felt, she was extremely immature, still a child; and that was charming. But then, of course, there was in the Dalloway family the tradition of public service — abbesses, principals, head mistresses, dignitaries[2], without any of them being brilliant.

She went a little further towards St. Paul's. She liked the geniality[3], sisterhood, motherhood, brotherhood of this noise. But it was later than she thought. Her mother would not like her to be wandering off alone like this. She turned back down the Strand. In spite of the heat, the wind was strong; it blew a thin black veil over the sun and the buildings.

Calmly and competently, Elizabeth Dalloway got on the Westminster omnibus.

1. bye-streets: 橫街
2. dignitaries: 傑出人物
3. geniality: 親切

Sentence-building

1 **Use these key words to make complete sentences and put the verbs in the correct tense.**

   1 age / Kilman / people / (not) dress / At / Miss / her / please/ to

   2 lady / When / want / Clarissa / cry / opposite / old / the / see / she / to

   3 feel / life / Miss / Mrs / that / her / waste / Kilman / Dalloway

   4 country / Elizabeth / alone / the / be left / much / in / prefer / to

Text Analysis

2 **Can you identify who is speaking?**

   1 'She should have been in a factory; behind a counter.'

   2 'You are taking Elizabeth to the Stores?'

   3 'All professions are open to women of your generation.'

   4 'You have such nice shoulders.'

   5 'I want to become either a farmer or a doctor!'

   6 'People don't ask me to parties.'

Grammar

3 **Look at these examples from Chapter Seven and re-write them in indirect speech, using the verb in CAPITALS.**

'Are you going to the party?' Miss Kilman said. ASK
Miss Kilman asked if she was going to the party.

1 Miss Kilman felt, Fool! You have wasted your life, Clarissa Dalloway. THINK

2 Clarissa leant over the bannisters and cried out to Elizabeth, 'Remember the party!' REMIND

3 'I never go to parties,' said Miss Kilman. INSIST

4 'Don't quite forget me,' said Doris Kilman to Elizabeth. ASK

5 Miss Kilman said to Elizabeth, 'I've not quite finished yet.' TELL

Grammar

4a **Look at these nouns from Chapter Seven. In the spaces, write the verbs formed from them.**

1 conversation _____
2 sufferings _____
3 pleasure _____
4 sight _____
5 breath _____

4b **Now write the adjectives next to these nouns.**

1 tradition _____
2 interest _____
3 sorrow _____
4 comforts _____
5 religion _____

Reading Comprehension

5 **Are these statements true (T) or false (F)?**

		T	F
1	Doris Kilman is as old as Mrs Dalloway.	☐	☐
2	Miss Kilman's family comes from Austria.	☐	☐
3	To Mrs Dalloway, Miss Kilman resembles a prehistoric monster.	☐	☐
4	Clarissa watches the old lady in the house opposite.	☐	☐
5	Elizabeth has ruined Miss Kilman's career.	☐	☐
6	Elizabeth enjoys sitting on top of the omnibus.	☐	☐
7	Elizabeth's ancestors were famous and brilliant.	☐	☐

Vocabulary & Writing

6a **How would you describe the atmosphere in this chapter? Find some adjectives from the text and put them inside the ellipse.**

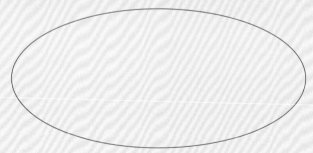

6b **Now write a short paragraph (50-80 words) in which you describe the atmosphere using the words you have found above.**

_____

_____

_____

_____

Use of English

7 Read these sentences from Chapter Seven and re-write them, using your own words.

1 Miss Dolby thought she would be happier with people who shared her views about the Germans.

_____

_____

2 Clarissa was really shocked. This woman had taken her daughter from her!

_____

_____

3 Somehow one respected that — that old woman looking out of the window, quite unconscious that she was being watched.

_____

_____

4 No Dalloways came down the Strand daily.

_____

_____

PRE-READING ACTIVITY

Reading Comprehension

8 Look at these words and phrases from Chapter Eight, then write their synonyms.

1 important street in West London
2 market
3 far away
4 suddenly came into the room
5 bumped into
6 thought about
7 writing
8 left

Chapter Eight

Impulsive Decisions

▶ 5 To Septimus Warren Smith, lying on the sofa in the sitting-room, the light and shadow made the wall grey, and the bananas bright yellow, and the Strand grey; and now the omnibuses bright yellow. The sound of water was in the room and the voices of birds singing came through the waves. His hand lay on the back of the sofa. Fear no more, says the heart in the body. He was not afraid.

Rezia, sitting at the table twisting[1] a hat in her hands, watched him; saw him smiling. He was happy. But she could not bear to see him smiling. It was not marriage — a husband who laughed, sat silently for hours, then told her to write; about war; about Shakespeare; about great discoveries; how there is no death. Sometimes he waved his hands and cried out that he knew the truth!

She wrote everything down. Once they discovered the girl who cleaned the room reading these papers and laughing. It was a terrible pity; it made Septimus cry out about human cruelty. He invented stories about Holmes — Holmes reading Shakespeare, roaring with laughter or rage[2], for Dr Holmes seemed to represent something horrible to him. 'Human nature,' he called him. Then there were the visions, and the music. 'Lovely!' he used to cry, and the tears would run down his cheeks; to Rezia it was dreadful[3] seeing brave Septimus,

1. **twisting:** 轉
2. **rage:** 狂怒
3. **dreadful:** 令人不快

who had fought in the War, crying.

She was making a hat for Mrs Filmer's married daughter, Mrs Peters. Rezia did not like her; but Mrs Filmer had been so good to them. 'She gave me grapes this morning,' she said — and Rezia wanted to do something to show that they were grateful.

Septimus began, very cautiously, to open his eyes. He looked at the sideboard[1], the plate of bananas; on the mantelpiece, with the jar of roses. None of these things moved. All were still; all were real. He shaded[2] his eyes so that he might see only a little of her face at a time, first the chin, then the nose, then the forehead. She was perfectly natural, with the pursed[3] lips and melancholy expression that women have when sewing.

'This hat's too small for Mrs Peters,' said Septimus. (Mrs Peters was a big woman.) 'Of course it was — absurdly small,' she said.

He took it out of her hands. He said it was an organ grinder's[4] monkey's hat. She was delighted! They hadn't laughed together like this for weeks! Never in her life had she felt so happy! She pinned a rose to the side of the hat. That was still more ridiculous, Septimus said. Now the poor woman looked like a pig at a fair. (Nobody ever made her laugh as Septimus did.)

She emptied her work-box on the table. He began putting strange colours together — for he had a wonderful eye[5], and often he was absurdly, wonderfully right.

'She shall have a beautiful hat!' he murmured. She must be very, very careful, he said, to keep it exactly as he had made it. So she sewed; he would wait, he thought.

'There it is,' said Rezia, turning Mrs Peters' hat on the tips of her

1. **sideboard:** 餐櫃的側板
2. **shaded:** 擋住
3. **pursed:** 撅嘴

4. **organ grinder's:** 街頭手風琴師的
5. **had a wonderful eye:** 視覺敏銳

fingers. It was wonderful. He was so proud. It would always make her happy to see that hat. He had become himself then, he had laughed. They had been alone together. Always she would like that hat.

He was very tired. He was very happy. He would sleep. He shut his eyes. But directly he saw nothing, the sounds of the cricket game became distant and strange and seemed like the cries of people seeking[1] and not finding. They had lost him!

He sat up, terrified. What did he see? The plate of bananas on the sideboard. Nobody was there (Rezia had gone out). He was alone with the sideboard and the bananas. 'Evans!' he cried. There was no answer.

Then Rezia burst into the room. She sat on the end of the sofa.

They were perfectly happy now, she said, suddenly. For she could say anything to him now. That was almost the first thing she had felt about him, that night in the café when he had come in with his English friends. He had come in, rather shyly, looking round him. She knew he was English; he was always thin; but he had a beautiful fresh colour; and with her he was always very gentle. Being older than she was and being so clever — how serious he was, wanting her to read Shakespeare before she could even read a child's story in English!— being so much more experienced, he could help her. And she too could help him.

But it was getting late. She wanted to know if, by moving the rose, she had improved the hat. As she sat there, waiting, he could feel her mind, like a bird, falling from branch to branch.

He remembered Sir William Bradshaw's words: 'The people we are most fond of are not good for us when we are ill.' Bradshaw said,

1. seeking: 尋找

he must be taught to rest. Bradshaw said they must be separated. 'Must,' 'must,' why 'must'? What power had Bradshaw over him? 'What right has Bradshaw to say 'must' to me?' he demanded.

'It is because you talked of killing yourself,' said Rezia. She brought him his papers, the things he had written, things she had written for him. They looked at them together on the sofa. Burn them! he cried. But Rezia laid her hands on them. Some were very beautiful, she thought. She would tie them up (for she had no envelope) with a piece of silk.

Even if they took him, she said, she would go with him. They could not separate them, she said.

'There!' she said. The papers were tied up. No one should get at them. She would put them away. Then she got up to go into the bedroom to pack their things, but hearing voices downstairs and thinking that Dr Holmes had perhaps called, ran down to prevent him coming up.

Septimus could hear her talking to Holmes on the staircase.

'My dear lady, I have come as a friend,' Holmes was saying.

'No. I will not allow you to see my husband,' she said.

But Holmes persevered[1]. 'My dear lady, allow me...' he said, putting her aside powerfully.

Holmes was coming upstairs. Holmes would burst open the door. Holmes would say, 'Having a panic attack?' Holmes would get him. But no; not Holmes; not Bradshaw. Getting up rather unsteadily[2], he considered Mrs Filmer's clean bread knife. No, I mustn't spoil that. The gas fire? But it was too late now. Holmes was coming. The last option was the large window; and the inconvenience of opening it

---

1. persevered: 堅持

2. unsteadily: 顫抖地

and throwing himself out. He sat on the sill[1]; he would wait till the very last moment. He did not want to die. Life was good. The sun was hot.

Holmes was at the door. 'I'll show you!' Septimus cried, and threw himself violently down on to Mrs Filmer's railings[2].

'The coward[3]!' cried Dr Holmes, breaking open the door. Rezia ran to the window, she saw; she understood. Dr Holmes and Mrs Filmer collided with each other. Mrs Filmer made Rezia hide her eyes in the bedroom. Dr Holmes came in — she must be brave and drink something, he said. Her husband was horribly mutilated[4], she must not see him. Who could have predicted it? A sudden impulse, no one was in the least to blame (he told Mrs Filmer).

As she drank, it seemed to Rezia that she was opening long windows, stepping out into some garden. But where? The clock was striking; she was falling asleep. She was running on a hill, somewhere near the sea; they sat on a cliff.

'He is dead,' she said, smiling at the poor old woman who guarded her with her honest light-blue eyes fixed on the door.

'Let her sleep,' said Dr Holmes, feeling her pulse[5]. She saw the large outline of his body standing dark against the window. So that was Dr Holmes.

❖ ❖ ❖

One of the triumphs of civilisation, Peter Walsh thought, as the bell of the ambulance sounded. The ambulance hurried to the hospital, having picked up instantly, humanely, some unfortunate person; someone hit on the head, attacked by disease, knocked over perhaps a minute ago at one of these crossings[6]. He noticed the efficiency, the

---

1. **sill:** 窗沿
2. **railings:** 欄杆
3. **coward:** 懦夫

4. **mutilated:** 受傷
5. **pulse:** 脈搏
6. **crossings:** 十字路口

organisation, the communal spirit of London. Every cart or carriage stopped to let the ambulance pass. Perhaps it was morbid[1], or perhaps touching, the respect which these busy people showed the ambulance with its victim inside.

One time he was riding with Clarissa on an omnibus somewhere; as they explored London, noticing strange scenes and people from the top of the bus, Clarissa said she felt herself everywhere; not 'here, here, here'; and she tapped the back of the seat; but everywhere. She waved her hand; she felt a strange sympathy with people she had never spoken to, some woman in the street, some man behind a counter — even trees. This feeling allowed her to believe that the invisible part of us survives after our death, and is somehow attached to some person or even haunts[2] certain places... perhaps.

Their long friendship of almost thirty years demonstrated Clarissa's theory. Their meetings had been brief, often painful; then there were his absences and the interruptions (this morning, for example, with Elizabeth coming in when he was talking to Clarissa); but the effect of them on his life was immeasurable. Clarissa had influenced him more than any person he had ever known, always cool, lady-like, critical, or magnificent, romantic...

He had reached his hotel. He crossed the hall and got his key off the hook. The young lady handed him some letters. He went upstairs.

Oh it was a letter from Clarissa! This blue envelope; that was her hand. And he would have to read it. Here was another of those meetings, certain to be painful! To read her letter was very difficult. 'How wonderful it was to see him. She must tell him that.' That was all.

1. **morbid:** 病態的
2. **haunts:** 作祟

But it upset him. It annoyed him. He wished she hadn't written it. Why couldn't she leave him alone? After all, she had married Dalloway, and lived with him in perfect happiness all these years.

To get that letter to him by six o'clock she must have sat down and written it immediately after he had left her; stamped it; sent somebody to the post. She was upset by his visit. For a moment possibly, when he kissed her hand, she had felt envy, regret; remembered possibly (for he saw her look it) something he had said — how they would change the world if she married him perhaps. But the reality was this: middle age, mediocrity[1]. As soon as he left her, she would be frightfully[2] sorry for him; she would think what she could do to give him pleasure (apart from the one thing which *would*) and he could see her with the tears running down her cheeks going to her writing-table and quickly putting, 'Wonderful to see you!' And she meant it.

But it would not have been a success, their marriage. The other thing, after all, came so much more naturally.

It was odd, actually, that HE, Peter Walsh, should have a contented look. This made him attractive to women who liked the sense that he was not completely manly. There was something unusual about him; he was bookish[3], he was a gentleman, which showed itself in his manners. He was a man — but not the sort of man one had to respect.

He pulled off his boots. He emptied his pockets. Out came with his pocket-knife a photograph of Daisy on the verandah[4], in white; very charming, the best he had ever seen of her. He could hear her now: of course she would give him everything, everything he wanted! (She had no sense of discretion[5].) And she was only twenty-four. And she had two children. Incredible!

1. **mediocrity:** 平庸
2. **frightfully:** 非常
3. **bookish:** 有書生氣質的

4. **verandah:** 門廊
5. **discretion:** 謹慎

As he walked silently around the room in his socks, he contemplated whether to go to Clarissa's party, or stay in and read an absorbing book written by a man he used to know at Oxford. There he was, the man Daisy thought the world of, the perfect gentleman, fascinating, distinguished (and his age made not the least difference to her), in a hotel room in Bloomsbury, shaving, washing. He never knew what people thought. It became more and more difficult for him to concentrate. Why couldn't Clarissa simply find him and Daisy somewhere to live and be nice to her; introduce her. And then he could just — just do what? Be alone, sufficient to himself; and yet nobody of course was more dependent upon others. And it would make him furious if Daisy loved anybody else! For he was jealous, uncontrollably jealous by temperament[1]. But where was his knife; and Clarissa's letter, which he would not read again but liked to think of, and Daisy's photograph? And now for dinner.

They were eating. Sitting at little tables, with their bags beside them, for they had been running about London all day shopping, sightseeing. They looked up as the nice-looking gentleman in spectacles[2] came in and took his seat at a little table by the curtain.

It was not that he said anything; it was his way of looking at the menu, of pointing to a particular wine, of sitting correctly at the table, that won him their respect.

He would go to Clarissa's party. He would go because he wanted to ask Richard what the Government intended to do about India[3].

He left his paper on the table and moved off. Here he was, starting to go to a party, at his age, believing that he was about to have an experience. But what?

1. by temperament: 性情
2. spectacles: 眼鏡

3. about India: 指印度爭取獨立

He walked through London, towards Westminster, observing. Was everybody having dinner out, then? Doors were being opened. Everybody was going out. It seemed as if the whole of London were getting into little boats and floating away in carnival.

And here was Clarissa's street; cabs were rushing round the corner, carrying, it seemed to him, people going to her party, Clarissa's party.

The brain must wake now. The body must contract[1] now, entering the lighted house, where the door stood open, where the motor cars were standing, and bright women descending: the soul must prepare to endure[2]. He opened the big blade of his pocket-knife.　■

1. contract: 縮小
2. endure: 啞忍

Reading Comprehension

1 **Are these statements true (T) or false (F)?**

T F

1 Rezia and Septimus laugh a lot about the hat for Mrs Filmer's daughter. ☐ ☐

2 Septimus still thinks a lot about his friend Evans. ☐ ☐

3 Rezia was advised to read children's stories to learn English. ☐ ☐

4 Septimus decides that he does not want Dr Holmes to get him. ☐ ☐

5 Peter Walsh knows why the ambulance is passing by. ☐ ☐

6 Peter receives a letter from Clarissa in a pink envelope. ☐ ☐

7 Daisy is twenty-four and has got two children. ☐ ☐

8 People at the hotel liked Peter's way of looking at the menu. ☐ ☐

Vocabulary

2a **Look at these nouns from Chapter Eight. In the spaces, write the adjectives formed from them.**

1 inconvenience _____

2 efficiency _____

3 regret _____

4 theory _____

5 envy _____

2b **Now write the nouns next to each of these adjectives.**

1 melancholy _____

2 brave _____

3 certain _____

4 upset _____

5 contented _____

Writing

3 Look back at Peter's reaction to Clarissa's letter (*'It annoyed him.'*). Imagine that he writes a reply — write in your exercise-book.

Sentence-building

4 Use these key words to make complete sentences putting the verbs in the correct tense.

1 Rezia / hat / proudly / tips / the / look / turn / the / her / at / of / Septimus / who / on / fingers

2 ambulance / When / Peter / to let / people / be / the / pass / impressed / stop

3 Clarissa / success / If / Peter / (not) be / would / marry / it / a

4 India / Richard / Peter / party / ask / so that / decide / Clarissa's / go / situation / in / to / about / the / he / could / Dalloway / to

Grammar

5 Look at these modal verb phrases from Chapter Eight. Can you link them to their meanings?

1 ☐ She must not see him.
2 ☐ ... so that he might only see a little of her face...
3 ☐ They could not separate them...
4 ☐ I mustn't spoil that.
5 ☐ Septimus could hear her talking...
6 ☐ She must tell him that.

a needs to...
b It is vital that she does not...
c ... was able to...
d ... have no right to...
e It was not right...
f in order to be able to

Vocabulary

6a Look at these words. The first is from the chapter you have just read; the other three are possible synonyms. Circle the one word which is NOT a synonym.

1 *absorbing*	ordinary	fascinating	entertaining
2 *immeasurable*	inconceivable	inestimable	immense
3 *sufficient*	enough	adequate	subtle
4 *brave*	courageous	bald	bold
5 *odd*	off	strange	weird

6b Now write down the odd word out, look it up in your dictionary or online and write an example sentence of your own.

_____

_____

_____

_____

_____

6c Now look at these verbs from the text. Look at the three possible synonym and circle the odd one out.

1 *tapped*	dug	knocked	rapped
2 *handed*	took off	gave	passed
3 *guarded*	watched over	kept an eye on	hesitated
4 *stepping out*	walking out	rushing out	moving out
5 *persevered*	persisted	gave up	kept on

6d Now write down the odd word out, look it up in your dictionary or online and write an example sentence of your own.

_____

_____

_____

_____

_____

Grammar

7 **Look at these examples from Chapter Eight and re-write them in indirect speech, using the verb in CAPITALS.**

"She shall have a beautiful hat," he murmured. THINK
He thought that she should have a beautiful hat.

1 'This hat's too small for Mrs Peters,' said Septimus. NOTICE

_____

2 'What right has Bradshaw to say 'must' to me?' he demanded. WONDER

_____

3 'My dear lady, I have come as a friend,' Holmes said. ASSURE

_____

4 'No, I will not allow you to see my husband,' she said. DECIDE

_____

5 'Let her sleep,' said Dr Holmes. INSIST

_____

PRE-READING ACTIVITY

Text Analysis

8 **Guess who says the following in Chapter Nine.**

1 'Oh dear, it is going to be a complete failure!'

_____

2 'I have five enormous boys.'

_____

3 'You look so like your mother, my dear.'

_____

4 'My husband was called up on the telephone, a very sad case.'

_____

5 'Where's the woman gone to?'

_____

6 'I looked at you and wondered, 'Who is that lovely girl?'.'

_____

Chapter Nine

Everything Comes Together

Lucy came running downstairs. She heard voices; people already coming up from dinner; she must fly!

The Prime Minister was coming, Agnes said: she had heard them say so in the dining-room, she said. It made no difference at this hour of the night to Mrs Walker: plates, saucepans, frying-pans, lemons and pudding bowls were everywhere, on the kitchen table, on chairs.

The ladies were going upstairs already, said Lucy; one by one, Mrs Dalloway walking last and sending back some message to the kitchen. There was laughter from the dining-room; the gentlemen were enjoying themselves when the ladies had gone.

Lucy said how Miss Elizabeth looked quite lovely; she couldn't take her eyes off her; in her pink dress, wearing the necklace Mr Dalloway had given her. There was a ring at the bell — and the gentlemen were still drinking in the dining-room! Ah, *now* they were going upstairs; they would come faster and faster, and the hall would be full of gentlemen waiting while the ladies took their cloaks off.

'Lady and Miss Lovejoy,' Mr Wilkins (hired[1] for parties) announced, 'Sir John and Lady Needham ... Miss Weld ... Mr Walsh.' His manner was admirable.

'How delightful to see you!' said Clarissa. She said it to everyone.

---

1. **hired:** 聘請兼職

She was at her worst — effusive[1], insincere. It was a great mistake to have come. He should have stayed at home and read his book, thought Peter Walsh; for he knew no one.

Oh dear, it was going to be a complete failure[2]; Clarissa felt it in her bones. She could see Peter out of the corner of her eye, criticising her, there, in that corner. Why, after all, did she do these things? It was extraordinary how Peter made her see herself. But why did he come, then, merely to criticise? Why always take, never give? Why not risk the little point of view one had? There he was, wandering off, and she must speak to him. But she would not get the chance. Life was that — humiliation, renunciation[3].

'Hullo, Richard,' said somebody, taking Dalloway by the elbow, and, good Lord, there was old Peter Walsh. He was delighted to see him — ever so pleased to see him! He hadn't changed a bit. And off they went together walking right across the room, giving each other little pats[4], as if they hadn't met for a long time.

The windows were open, and now the yellow curtain blew out. And Clarissa saw Ralph Lyon push it back, and go on talking. So the party wasn't a complete failure after all! It was going to be all right now. It had started.

And yet for her, it was too much work. She was not enjoying it. Anybody could just stand there. Every time she gave a party she had this feeling of being something not herself, and that everyone was unreal.

They came up the stairs one after another — oh, Lady Bruton! 'How awfully good of you to come!' she said, and she meant it. WHAT name? Lady Rosseter? But who on earth was Lady Rosseter?

---

1. **effusive:** 過於熱情
2. **failure:** 這裏指災難
3. **renunciation:** 放棄
4. **pats:** 輕拍

'Clarissa!' That voice! It was Sally Seton! After all these years!

It was extraordinary to see her again, older, happier, less lovely. They kissed each other on the cheek, by the drawing-room door, and Clarissa turned, with Sally's hand in hers, and saw her rooms full, heard all the voices, the blowing curtains, and the roses which Richard had given her.

'I have five enormous boys,' said Sally.

'I can't believe it!' Clarissa cried; but Wilkins wanted her; Wilkins announced, in a voice of commanding authority, one name:

'The Prime Minister,' said Peter Walsh.

The Prime Minister? Was it really? He looked so ordinary. But, as he went round, first with Clarissa then with Richard, he did his job very well. He tried to look somebody. It was amusing to watch. Nobody looked at him. They just went on talking, yet it was perfectly clear that they all knew and felt this symbol of what they all stood for[1], English society. Old Lady Bruton, looking very fine, approached the Prime Minister and they disappeared into a little room which was at once observed, guarded. Good Lord, the snobbery of the English! thought Peter Walsh, standing in the corner. How they love showing their respect! And there's Hugh Whitbread, grown rather fatter, rather whiter, the admirable Hugh! Look at him now, bowing[2], as the Prime Minister and Lady Bruton came out of that room, saying something private to Lady Bruton as she passed.

Now Clarissa took her Prime Minister down the room, dancing, sparkling[3], with her elegant grey hair, ear-rings and a silver-green dress. There was a breath of tenderness; an exquisite cordiality[4]; as if she wished the whole world well. So she made Peter think.

---

1. **stood for:** 代表
2. **bowing:** 鞠躬
3. **sparkling:** 發光，這裏指精力充沛
4. **cordiality:** 有禮

(But he was not in love.)

Indeed, Clarissa felt, the Prime Minister had been good to come. And, walking down the room with him, with Sally there and Peter there and Richard very pleased, she had felt that intoxication of the moment. But these triumphs (dear old Peter, for example, thinking her so brilliant), were hollow; perhaps she was growing old but they did not satisfy her as they used to.

'Dear Clarissa!' exclaimed old Mrs Hilbery. She looked tonight, Mrs Hilbery said, so like her mother as she first saw her walking in a garden in a grey hat. Clarissa's eyes filled with tears. Her mother, walking in a garden!

But unfortunately, she must go. She must speak to that couple, said Clarissa, Lord Gayton and Nancy Blow.

THEY did not add perceptibly[1] to the noise of the party. They were not talking (perceptibly) as they stood side by side by the yellow curtains. They looked (that was enough) so clean and healthy. Mrs Dalloway came up. Lord Gayton liked her immensely. So did Miss Blow. She had such charming manners.

'It is delicious of you to have come!' Clarissa said. 'I had meant to have dancing,' she added.

For the young people could not talk. And why should they? The power of the English language, to communicate feelings (at their age, she and Peter would have been arguing all the evening), was not for them. But talk of dancing! The rooms were packed.

There was old Aunt Helena, old Miss Parry, in her shawl[2]. For Miss Helena Parry was not dead: she was alive. She was past eighty. She climbed the stairs slowly with a stick. She was placed in a chair

1. **perceptibly:** 明顯地
2. **shawl:** 圍巾

(Richard had organised that). It was tiring; it was noisy; but Clarissa had asked her. So she had come. It was a pity that Richard and Clarissa lived in London — if only for Clarissa's health, it would have been better to live in the country. But Clarissa had always been fond of society.

Clarissa must speak to Lady Bruton. 'Richard so much enjoyed his lunch party,' she said to Lady Bruton.

'Richard helped me to write a letter,' Lady Bruton replied. 'And how are you?'

'Oh, perfectly well!' said Clarissa. (Lady Bruton detested illness in the wives of politicians.)

'And there's Peter Walsh!' said Lady Bruton (for she could never think of anything to say to Clarissa; though she liked her). She shook hands with him; stood by Miss Parry's chair; invited him to lunch. She would like to have Peter Walsh's opinion on the situation in India.

But was it Lady Bruton (whom she used to know)? Was it Peter Walsh grown grey? Lady Rosseter (who had been Sally Seton) asked herself. It was old Miss Parry certainly — the old aunt who used to be so angry when she stayed at Bourton. And oh, Clarissa! Sally caught her by the arm.

Clarissa stopped beside them. 'But I can't stay,' she said. 'I shall come later. Wait,' she said, looking at Peter and Sally. They must wait, she meant, until all these people had gone.

'I shall come back,' she said, looking at her old friends, Sally and Peter, who were shaking hands, and Sally, remembering the past, was laughing.

Her voice had lost its richness, her eyes their brightness; but everybody adored her, her warmth; her vitality[1]. And Clarissa

1. vitality: 朝氣

remembered her melodramatic[1] love of being the centre of everything. And now she was married to a bald man who reportedly owned cotton mills at Manchester. And she had five boys!

She and Peter had settled down together. They were talking: it seemed so familiar — that they should be talking. They would discuss the past. With the two of them (more even than with Richard) she shared her past. But she must leave them. There were the Bradshaws, whom she disliked. She must go up to Lady Bradshaw and say…

But Lady Bradshaw anticipated her.

'We are shockingly late, dear Mrs Dalloway, we almost did not come,' she said.

And Sir William, who looked very distinguished, with his grey hair and blue eyes, said yes; they had not been able to resist the temptation. He looked what he was, a great doctor. Clarissa watched as Sir William talked to Richard. She did not know what it was — about Sir William; what exactly she disliked. Only Richard agreed with her, 'didn't like his taste, didn't like his smell.'

In a low voice Lady Bradshaw murmured how, 'just as we were starting, my husband was called up on the telephone, a very sad case. A young army man had killed himself.' Oh! thought Clarissa, in the middle of my party, here's death, she thought.

She went on, into the little room where the Prime Minister had gone with Lady Bruton. Perhaps there was somebody there. But there was nobody.

What business[2] had the Bradshaws to talk of death at her party? A young man had killed himself. And they talked of it at her party. He had killed himself — but how? He had thrown himself from a

1. melodramatic: 誇張
2. business: 這裏指理由、資格

window. But why had he done it?

Death was defiance[1]. Death was an attempt to communicate; people feeling the impossibility of reaching the centre which, mystically, escaped them. 'If it were now to die, 'twere now to be most happy,' she had said to herself once.

She walked to the window, parted[2] the curtains and looked. How surprising!— in the room opposite the old lady stared straight at her! She was going to bed. It was fascinating to watch that old lady moving about, crossing the room, coming to the window. Could she see her? It was fascinating, with people still laughing and shouting in the drawing-room, to watch that old woman, quietly, going to bed. She pulled the blind now. The clock began striking. The young man had killed himself; but she did not pity him. The words came to her, Fear no more the heat of the sun. She must go back to her guests. But what an extraordinary night! She felt somehow very like the young man who had killed himself. She felt glad that he had done it; thrown it away. She must find Sally and Peter. And she came in from the little room.

'But where is Clarissa?' said Peter. He was sitting on the sofa with Sally. 'Where's the woman gone to?' he asked.

That was his old trick, thought Sally, always opening and shutting a pocket-knife when he got excited. She and Peter Walsh had been very intimate when he was in love with Clarissa. Then Peter had gone off to India, and she had heard about an unhappy marriage, and she didn't know whether he had any children, and she couldn't ask him, for he had changed. He was kinder, she felt, and she had a real affection for him, for he was connected with her youth.

1. **defiance:** 反抗
2. **parted:** 打開

Sally owed Clarissa an enormous amount. They had been friends, not acquaintances. But — did Peter understand? — she lacked something. She had extraordinary charm. But to be frank (and she felt that Peter was an old friend), how could Clarissa have married Richard Dalloway? a sportsman, a man who cared only for dogs.

Where was she, all this time? It was getting late.

Poor Peter, thought Sally. Why did Clarissa not come and talk to them? That was what he wanted more than anything. She knew it. All the time he was thinking only of Clarissa, and was fidgeting with[1] his knife.

He had not found life simple, Peter said. His relations with Clarissa had not been simple. It had spoilt his life, he said. One could not be in love twice, he said. And what could she say? Still, it is better to have loved.

Clarissa had cared for him more than she had ever cared for Richard. Sally was positive of that.

'No, no, no!' said Peter (Sally should not have said that — that was too much).

When one was young, said Peter, one was too excited to know people. Now that one was old, fifty-two to be precise, said Peter (Sally was fifty-five, in body, she said, but her heart was like a girl's of twenty), one could watch, one could understand, and one did not lose the power of feeling, he said. No, that is true, said Sally. She felt more deeply, more passionately, every year.

There's Elizabeth, he said, she does not feel half what we feel, not yet. But, said Sally, watching Elizabeth go across the room to her father, one can see they are devoted to[2] each other.

---

1. **fidgeting with:** 玩弄
2. **devoted to:** 這裏指愛、對彼此堅貞

For her father had been looking at her, as he stood talking to the Bradshaws, and he had thought, Who is that lovely girl? And suddenly he realised that it was his Elizabeth. They stood together, now that the party was almost over, and the rooms were getting emptier and emptier. Richard was proud of his daughter. And he had not meant to tell her, but he could not help telling her. He had looked at her, he said, and he had wondered, Who is that lovely girl? and it was his daughter! That did make her happy.

'Richard has improved. You are right,' said Sally. 'I shall go and talk to him. I shall say goodnight. What does the brain matter,' said Lady Rosseter, getting up, 'compared with the heart?'

'I will come,' said Peter, but he stayed seated for a moment. What is this terror? What is this ecstasy? he thought to himself. What is it that fills me with extraordinary excitement?

It is Clarissa, he said.

For there she was.

Vocabulary

1a **Look at these verbs from Chapter Nine. In the spaces, write the nouns formed from them.**

1 enjoy _____

2 laugh _____

3 murmur _____

4 criticise _____

5 dislike _____

6 anticipate _____

1b **Now do the same with these adjectives from the text. Write their nouns next to each one.**

1 intimate _____

2 devoted _____

3 precise _____

4 charming _____

Reading Comprehension

2 **Are these statements true (T) or false (F)?**

		T	F
1	Peter does not like the way Clarissa greets her guests.	☐	☐
2	Clarissa is surprised to see Sally at her party.	☐	☐
3	Nobody is interested in the Prime Minister.	☐	☐
4	Clarissa is crying because she doesn't want to look like her mother.	☐	☐
5	Old Aunt Helena has been invited to Clarissa's party.	☐	☐
6	Clarissa tells Peter and Sally that she will talk to them later.	☐	☐
7	Peter opens and shuts his pocket-knife when he is bored.	☐	☐
8	Seeing Clarissa makes Peter happy.	☐	☐

Grammar

3 **Look at these examples from Chapter Nine and re-write them in indirect speech, using the verb in CAPITALS.**

'How delightful to see you!' said Clarissa to everyone. TELL
Clarissa told everyone how delightful it was to see them.

1 'How awfully good of you to come!' she said. REMARK

2 'I can't believe it!' Clarissa cried. REPLY

3 'Richard so much enjoyed his lunch party,' she said. BE CONVINCED

4 'But I can't stay,' she said. DECIDE

5 'But where is Clarissa?' said Peter. WONDER

Vocabulary

4a **Look at these words. The first adjective is from the chapter you have just read; the other three are possible synonyms. Circle the one word which is NOT a synonym.**

1	*amusing*	entertaining	funny	annoying
2	insincere	critical	dishonest	artificial
3	delighted	thrilled	ecstatic	pleasing
4	distinguished	different	respected	notable
5	extraordinary	exceptional	supernatural	tremendous
6	delicious	lovely	delightful	delirious

4b **Now write down the odd word out, look it up in your dictionary or online and write an example sentence of your own.**

Virginia Woolf
Life and Times

Virginia with her mother

Virginia with her father

Virginia with her sister Vanessa Bell

A Stimulating Childhood

Virginia Woolf was born on 25 January, 1882 into an upper-middle-class literary family in Victorian London. The family lived near Hyde Park and had a busy social life involving artists, writers, politicians and aristocrats. Virginia was educated at home and she became an enthusiastic reader of her father's books. She soon decided that she wanted to be a writer.

Death and Its Effects

By the age of 24, Virginia had suffered four deaths in the family which were to have a significant effect on her health for the rest of her life. Her mother Julia died when Virginia was only 13 years old; two years later, her half-sister Stella Duckworth died suddenly. Virginia's father died in 1904 after a long illness and then two years later her brother Thoby died while travelling in Greece. Virginia was obsessed with the memory of her dead parents; she wrote a portrait of them in her 1927 novel *To The Lighthouse*. She suffered a mental breakdown after her mother died and again after her father's death, when she attempted to commit suicide for the first time.

Lively Evenings

In 1904, Virginia, her sister Vanessa and their two brothers moved to the west central area of London known as Bloomsbury. They and their brothers' Cambridge University friends formed The Bloomsbury Group, inviting artists and students to get together at Virginia's house on Thursday evenings to discuss such topics as religion, sex and art. For Virginia, these weekly meetings made up for the undergraduate education which Victorian society had refused to give her.

Marriage and Publishing

Virginia with her husband Leonard Woolf

In 1912 Virginia married one of her brother's university friends, Leonard Woolf, a civil servant. After their marriage, he became an independent intellectual and writer. In 1915, Virginia's first novel, *The Voyage Out*, was published and two years later, she and Leonard founded The Hogarth Press, which in time would become an important publisher of works by such authors as Katherine Mansfield, Sigmund Freud and T.S. Eliot.

A New Kind of Novel

After the First World War, Virginia looked for a written style which would reflect the chaos and insecurity of post-war England. When *Mrs Dalloway* was published in 1925, it presented readers with an experimental technique known as "stream of consciousness" — depicting a world in which characters experience events and sensations, then change their minds or remember things differently; a world in which reality is different for each person... all within the everyday context of shopping, having lunch, going for a walk and preparing for a party.

Success, Illness... and The End

Although Virginia continued to struggle with mental illness, she had a busy social life, much like Clarissa Dalloway. Four more novels — *To The Lighthouse*, *Orlando*, *The Waves* and *The Years* — were published in her lifetime and one, *Between The Acts*, appeared posthumously. Soon after she had completed the manuscript of this last work, Virginia became too ill to work. On 28 March 1941, she went to the River Ouse near her Sussex country home and walked into the water, her pockets full of stones. Her body was found only three weeks later. "Dearest," she wrote in a note to Leonard, "I feel certain that I am going mad again ... And I shan't recover this time ... So I am doing what seems the best thing to do."

The Aftermath of World War One

'The European War — that little game for schoolboys with explosives?'

Before the First World War of 1914-18, Europe believed that its political institutions were solid and rational. The British Empire had been a "global mission" to progress and to civilise. But the global conflict which cost the lives of nine million soldiers changed everything; instead of representing European advancement and superiority, The Great War, as it became known, was seen as an example of the most primitive and destructive feelings of hatred and anger. In England, confidence in the Empire was lost and people felt that "civilisation" now meant animal-like brutality towards fellow human beings. It was far from being just a game for schoolboys with explosives.

'The War was over, thank Heaven.'

Virginia Woolf and her circle of intellectual friends in *The Bloomsbury Group* were active pacifists throughout the four years of the war and inevitably they were shocked by its after-effects on society. The confidence of the English ruling class was shattered and post-war England began a new age of self-doubt and scepticism.

Mrs Dalloway is set in 1923, five years after the end of the conflict, and when, at the beginning of the novel, Clarissa observes with relief that "the War was over, thank Heaven", her comment reveals how slow society was in learning the lessons of the horror. Septimus Warren Smith is a war veteran who is still tortured by visions of his dead friend Evans and of the fighting. His doctor declares that there is nothing the matter with him and encourages Rezia to get Septimus interested in "things outside himself". This refusal by Dr Holmes to accept the traumatic effects of war on the individual is Virginia Woolf's way of ridiculing a bigger, more serious illness: society's own denial that something had changed for ever.

Members of the Bloomsbury Group gathering together

A Generation Threatened

Septimus Warren Smith is the literary example of what became known as "the Lost Generation" — a term for all those men who fought in The Great War and who never recovered from the experience. The politicians of the time, however, concentrated on another threat to society: the possibility of future aggression against Britain. After the technological developments in World War One of poison gas and attacks from the air, people began to panic about the number of deaths if another war broke out. Civilians felt that they were no longer safe — and so the British diplomatic card of negotiation by "appeasement" was played whenever international disagreements arose and acts of aggression happened. Most famously, this "softer" approach was to prove catastrophic in the late 1930s, when British Prime Minister Neville Chamberlain negotiated with Adolf Hitler in the run-up to the outbreak of World War Two. Trauma, uncertainty, fear and panic — these were the dramatic sentiments which the First World War had created in a world far removed from the comfortable existence of the Edwardian era at the beginning of the 20th century.

The Style of *Mrs Dalloway*

What Happens?

Anyone who reads *Mrs Dalloway* might say that the story does not contain much excitement; only at the end of the novel does something dramatic happen to one of the characters. By the final pages, we have returned to the safe social context of Clarissa's high-society party. There is no traditional resolution to the questions raised by the people in this story — the focus simply returns to the central character of Clarissa, observed as the "perfect hostess": *"For there she was."* The main emphasis in *Mrs Dalloway* is on the thoughts of the characters rather than their actions.

Vanessa Bell selfportrait

Which Point of View?

In 1925, Virginia Woolf wrote in an essay: *"In the vast catastrophe of the European war, our emotions had to be broken up for us, and put at an angle from us."* Mrs Dalloway presents what Woolf called "moments of being" — personal impressions of life which the characters experience at various moments of their day. Emotions change from happiness to fear, from nervousness to frustration, from anger to desperation. This technique is "stream of consciousness": multiple points of view, the interior thoughts of major and minor characters, which often flow together. Clarissa Dalloway, for example, is seen through the eyes of several characters: her husband Richard Dalloway, her former lover Peter Walsh, her friend Sally Seton and her daughter's history teacher Miss Kilman. There are even momentary impressions of her by less important characters. By the end of the book, we are left with a kaleidoscope of impressions of Clarissa.

Which Time?

A rich and varied element of *Mrs Dalloway* is how time is presented. All the characters are given a past, which comes from individual memories. Virginia Woolf talked in her diary in 1923 about how she constructed past lives for her characters: *"I dig out beautiful caves behind my characters. The idea is that the caves shall connect and each comes to daylight at the present moment."* Often the past represents a crossroads where important decisions have been taken which influence lives — often resulting in the nostalgic view, "What if I had done it differently...?" Present time is shown subjectively through the characters' "stream of consciousness" and objectively through the chimes of Big Ben, which serve as a dramatic reminder of reality for the characters.

Thinking and Talking

Virginia Woolf uses free indirect speech, which allows her either to express the interior monologue of the character or to represent closely what the person says and often to ridicule them. When Clarissa rests after visiting the florist's, the reader "hears" her thoughts about her life and knows that these are only happening inside her head. When Rezia asks Dr Holmes for medical advice about Septimus's condition, Woolf exposes the doctor's superior tone when he says *"for did he not owe his own excellent health ... to the fact that he could switch off?"*; she is equally critical of Sir William Bradshaw's behaviour towards Rezia: *"If Mrs Warren Smith was quite sure she had no more questions to ask — he never hurried his patients — they would return to her husband."* The style of free indirect speech highlights the impressionistic universe of the book and its characters.

The Genesis of *Mrs Dalloway*

Virginia Woolf described *Mrs Dalloway* as "a study of insanity and suicide." The world of postwar London is seen through the subjective eyes and thoughts of a variety of characters, sane (Clarissa) and insane (Septimus), rational (Richard) and irrational (Sir William Bradshaw).

Woolf's diary entry for October 1922 recorded that she had decided to write a series of short stories featuring Clarissa Dalloway — a character introduced to readers in Woolf's first novel *The Voyage Out* (1915) — and culminating in her party at home. Virginia herself enjoyed giving parties as part of her and Leonard Woolf's active social life and she wanted to examine how people feel at such an event and how they interact with other guests. Leonard said that she was excited by "the rise of temperature of mind and body" and "the ferment and fountain of noise". Then Woolf changed her mind and decided instead to write a more serious, full-length novel. She gave the project the working title of *The Hours*.

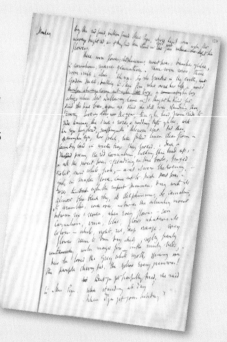

At one point Virginia Woolf intended Clarissa to die at the end of the party, possibly by suicide. But then she introduced a principal character, Septimus, as a way of presenting the theme of madness in the book. In a diary entry for June 1923, Woolf said that she wanted to "give life & death, sanity & insanity; I want to criticise the social system, & to show it at work, at its most intense."

Although Septimus is the one character who is most obviously suffering from a mental disorder, Peter Walsh and Miss Kilman display erratic and irrational behaviour during the day described in the book. Even Clarissa herself suffers from moments of intense insecurity — she worries about her age and the success of her party and she questions the value of her existence. Woolf said it was a world "seen by the sane and the insane, side by side."

When Rezia decides that her husband Septimus needs medical attention, the reactions of Dr Holmes and Sir William Bradshaw represent a complete lack of understanding and compassion. Virginia Woolf uses the opportunity to expose the medical profession's refusal to recognise the effects on soldiers of the First World War. This closely mirrors Virginia Woolf's own treatment by her appropriately named personal physician, Dr Savage.

Clarissa Dalloway and Septimus Warren Smith never meet, although Sir William Bradshaw "connects" them when he tells Clarissa at her party of Septimus's fateful action. Initially Clarissa is angry at Sir William; then she begins to contemplate what Septimus has done and in the end she applauds his action as "an attempt to communicate". In their separate existences, Clarissa and Septimus mirror each other: both believe that life no longer has meaning, both feel isolated from the world and from the person each of them has married. Both contemplate death at some point in the timeframe of the novel: one chooses a party as a way of revitalising oneself, the other chooses a more definitive way of escaping reality.

A young reader

TEST YOURSELF 自測

1 Think about your response to *Mrs Dalloway*. Which aspects of the novel did you enjoy? How does it hold the reader's attention? Where in the novel is there the "... humanity, humour, depth ... " (Diary, 30 August 1923) that Virginia Woolf said she wanted?

2 In her 1919 essay Modern Fiction, Virginia Woolf wrote: 'Examine for a moment an ordinary mind on an ordinary day'. In what ways does *Mrs Dalloway* represent this examination?

3 Is there a clear narrator at any point in *Mrs Dalloway*, or does Virginia Woolf just give us the thoughts of the various characters?

4 Clarissa Dalloway and Septimus Warren Smith never meet — but Septimus's action at the end of the novel "touches" Clarissa profoundly. How does she find a connection with what he does, and how do the two characters reflect each other?

5 Write an assessment of the character of Peter Walsh, considering his past and how he behaves and thinks on his return to London.

6 In Chapter Eight, Peter Walsh recalls Clarissa saying that "... the invisible part of us survives after our death, and is somehow attached to some person or even haunts certain places... ". How important a part of Clarissa's character is this kind of observation? Do you believe that something continues after death?

7 Watch the film version of *Mrs Dalloway* (1997) and make notes on the differences between the book and the film. Which do you prefer?

8 In 1998 the American author Michael Cunningham wrote *The Hours*, which takes Virginia Woolf's working title for the novel. The action has three timelines: 1920s London, with Woolf starting to write *Mrs Dalloway*, 1940s Los Angeles, where a young wife and mother is reading the novel; and 1990s New York, where a woman is preparing for a party for a friend. Read the novel and/or watch the Oscar-winning film of 2003, and think about the parallels with Woolf's original work.

SYLLABUS 語法重點和學習主題

Verbs:
Past Simple
Past Continuous
Present Perfect Simple and Continuous
Past Perfect Simple and Continuous
Future *will* and going to
Phrasal verbs

Modal verbs:
Could/could have (past ability)
Should/should have
Will/shall
Would/would have (habitual action/future in the past)
Might/might have (future/present/past possibility)
Must/must have (obligation/past deduction)
Must not (prohibition)
Need not (necessity)

Others:
Free indirect speech

Like

If clauses (zero, 1-2-3)

Had better

Gerund

As if
Even if/Even though/Although
If only...

Be about to

So/so that (result)

Relative clauses with *which* and *who*

As (time clause)
By (time)

Answer Key 答案

//

Mrs Dalloway

Pages 6-7

1 *Suggested words:* dancing, food, gossip, guests, dinner, music, elegant (clothes), wine, cars, taxis, smoking, Lords/Ladies,

2-4 Personal answers

5 *Suggested anwer:* Clarissa thinks about her limited education, how little she knows about the world and how there is so much going on in it that it is frightening and dangerous to try to get through just one day.

6 *Suggested answer:* The author wants the book to be about Clarissa Dalloway herself, not about something external like her party. She uses the event as a means of showing us various sides to Clarissa's personality and her interaction with some of the other characters in the novel.

Pages 18-21

1 1 F 2 F 3 T 4 T 5 T 6 F 7 F 8 T

2 (1) decided (2) choose (3) walked (4) thought (5) had refused (6) was (7) assured (8) would be (9) heard (10) carrying (11) drove (12) sit (13) stared (14) realised (15) missed (16) flying (17) poured out

3 1 Clarissa Dalloway (on meeting Hugh Whitbread in St James's Park) 2 Miss Pym (in the florist's) 3 Septimus Warren Smith (to his wife Rezia) 4 Hugh Whitbread (to Clarissa) 5 Maisie Johnson 6 Rezia Warren Smith

4 *Suggestions:*

Clarissa's Past	Clarissa's Present	Clarissa's Future
- Bourton, as a girl of 18 - serious (something terrible going to happen?) - Hugh Whitbread - not marrying Peter Walsh	- walks to florist's - loves life, activity in London, this time of year - considers her daughter Elizabeth's relationship with Miss Kilman - believes she knows who is in the dove-grey car	- she will "survive" after her death - hopes Elizabeth will stop her friendship with Miss Kilman

5 1 Rezia was worried that people might have heard Septimus saying/announcing that he would kill himself. 2 Dr Holmes wanted Rezia to encourage Septimus to become interested in the outside world. 3 Clarissa really wanted to have the same attitude as Richard, who did things for their essential value. 4 Clarissa wondered whether it was important that she would die and that everything would continue without her.

6 Personal answers

7 *Suggested ideas:* Both Clarissa and Septimus feel isolated and alone in their marriage and there is a similar distance from their respective partners. For Clarissa, it is Richard's political career and his character which have caused this; for Septimus, the lasting effects of the First World War have resulted in his alienation from Rezia. Richard is portrayed as being less passionate than Peter Walsh, whom Clarissa *could* have married but chose not to; Rezia is a passionate Italian woman who feels displaced amongst the English.

8-9 Personal answers

10 1 F 2 F 3 T 4 F 5 T 6 F 7 F 8 T

Pages 32-35

1 **1** Lucy said, "Can I help to mend that dress?" **2** Mrs Dalloway said, "You have enough on your hands already." **3** Peter said, "I only reached London last night. I will have to go to the country at once." **4** Clarissa said, "Do you mind my just finishing what I am doing to my dress? For we have a party tonight." **5** Peter said, "The lawyers and solicitors are going to do it."

2 **CLARISSA**
blessed, purified, (suddenly) aged, cold with excitement, (face) delicate, glad, shy, shocked, embarrassed, alone, (voice) frail, thin, far away
SALLY
extraordinary beauty, dark, large-eyed, abandonment, powerful personality, (voice) beautiful

3 **1** Sally Seton, while staying at Bourton; the guests go outside and then Sally kisses Clarissa. **2** Peter Walsh, arriving unexpectedly at the Dalloways' house; he goes into the drawing-room and surprises Clarissa. **3** Elizabeth, interrupting Clarissa and Peter Walsh's discussion in the drawing-room; Peter rushes out, saying goodbye, and leaves. **4** Lucy, trying to give Mrs Dalloway a message; Clarissa reads the message on her telephone pad. **5** Clarissa, complimenting Lucy; she gives her an old cushion to get rid of.

4 (*Missing words in* ***bold***) **1** When Clarissa realised that she had not been invited **to** lunch **by** Lady Bruton, she tried not **to** feel disappointed. **2** Clarissa wondered about the difference **between** falling in love with a man and with a woman. **3** Clarissa stopped **at** the top of the stairs to listen to the preparations **for** her party. **4** Clarissa could not believe **her** eyes when her old friend Peter Walsh came **in(to)** the room. **5** Peter became more and more irritated **at/by** Clarissa because **of** her situation and lifestyle. **6** Peter ran **out of** the room when Elizabeth interrupted his conversation **with** Clarissa.

5 **1** Clarissa feels disappointed about not being invited to Lady Bruton's luncheon and she also feels lonely, particularly now that she usually rests and sleeps in the attic room, as instructed by Richard and by her doctor. This small room is now at the heart of her life – and she feels its emptiness.
2 Clarissa has just mentioned her party to Peter; he has put out his hand to her and then pulled back. Now she looks at him, thinking about their shared past (at Bourton) and she is not sure exactly which emotion she is experiencing, now that he has suddenly reappeared: is it regret at what did not happen between them (marriage), or relief, or something she has not felt for a very long time. Whatever the emotion, it makes her look at him *"doubtfully"*.
3 At an extremely emotional moment in their surprise meeting, Peter asks Clarissa directly whether she is happy in her marriage to Richard – but he is about to be interrupted in the next instant by the arrival of Clarissa's daughter, Elizabeth. Peter will then leave in a hurry, leaving their conversation unfinished.
4 Clarissa was aware of feeling her age in Chapter One and here again she thinks about how old she is – especially just after remembering times at Bourton. This time, however, she is momentarily positive – immediately before this thought, she says to herself *"She was not old yet"*.
5 Clarissa is remembering Sally Seton's character from her days at Bourton; she indirectly compares herself to Sally by recalling her ability to say and do anything (*"abandonment"*). There is a tone of regret here, perhaps also envy.

6 **1** T **2** F **3** T **4** F **5** T (*possible interpretation*) **6** F **7** F (*"And then in a second it was over."*) **8** T

7 **CLARISSA:** hard, sentimental, insincere, cold, arrogant, unimaginative, maternal
RICHARD: awkward
PETER: emotional, empty, sad, happy
THE WOMAN: attractive, young, enchanting, delightful
ELIZABETH: strange-looking, big, grown-up, handsome

Pages 46-49

1 **1** Peter **decided** that Elizabeth was strange-looking and that she couldn't be more than eighteen. **2** Sally Seton **asked** whether it made any real difference to one's feelings to know that before they'd married she had had a baby. **3** Peter **was convinced** that she/Clarissa would marry that man/Richard. **4** Peter **insisted** on Clarissa telling him the truth./Peter insisted that Clarissa tell him the truth. **5** Clarissa **told** Peter that it was no use; it/that was the end. **6** Peter **made up his mind** that he would try and speak to Elizabeth alone that night.

2 **1** Peter, referring to Clarissa's character – how it has changed from when he knew her at Bourton to now, in her married life with Richard Dalloway. **2** In Trafalgar Square: Peter has seen an *"extraordinarily attractive"* young woman and he has decided to follow her – without intending to approach her and talk to her. **3** Peter is remembering Regent's Park as a child, which surprises him as a man, since he believes that it is women who are more attached to what has happened in the past and where. **4** Peter is dreaming in Regent's Park. His dream is about a *"solitary traveller journeying through a forest"*. **5** In Bourton, summer: Clarissa has just reacted very snobbishly to a story about a man who had married his housemaid. Her mood changes dramatically when she sees her dog. **6** In Bourton, summertime, at dinner: Clarissa has just talked to Peter *"as if they had never met before"*, like the perfect hostess he has always said she would become. He thinks about this and recognises her social skills. **7** In Bourton, after dinner: Clarissa and her friends decide to go boating. She goes back inside the house to fetch Peter – and he is delighted at *"her generosity – her goodness"*. **8** In Bourton: the scene at the fountain, when Clarissa tells Peter that their intimate friendship is over.

3 **1** weep **2** feel **3** move

4 **1** T **2** F – Clarissa and a few other people know that he is back. **3** F – if she stops, he will ask her to go and have an ice-ream with him. **4** T **5** F – Peter falls asleep. **6** T **7** T **8** F – he felt as if she had hit him in the face.

5 B, E, D, F, H, A, G, C

6 *(Suggested version in the Present, although can be in the Past)*
Peter Walsh **leaves** Clarissa's house and **wonders** why Clarissa spends her time **giving** parties. He **believes** that she **has become** conventional in her middle age. He also **feels** embarrassed about **weeping** at Clarissa's.
A group of teenage boys **marches** past him and he **tries** to **keep** up with them. Then he **sees** a beautiful young woman and **decides** to **follow** her. When she **goes** inside her house, Peter **walks** to Regent's Park to **find** a bench on which to **relax**. He **falls** asleep. He **wakes** up and **thinks** about the time at Bourton when Clarissa **rejects** him.

7 **BEFORE THE WAR**: innocent, lean- and hostile-faced, shy, stammering, anxious, weakly-looking
AFTER THE WAR: the happiest and most miserable man in the world, half-educated and self-educated, mechanical, melodramatic, insincere

8 Personal answers

Pages 60-63

1 *(Missing words in **bold**)* **1** Lucrezia decided **to** go back **to** Milan so that **she** would not suffer any more. **2** After five years away **in** India, Peter noticed how people behaved differently. **3** Nobody believed that Hugh Whitbread had kissed the penniless Sally Seton **in the** smoking-room! **4 At** work, Mr. Brewer wanted Septimus **to** stay healthy by taking up football. **5 In** Italy, Rezia liked **the** English because they were so silent. **6** Dr Holmes refused **to** accept that Septimus was ill **and** said **that** there was nothing **the** matter.

2 **1** Rezia could not take/tolerate it any longer. **2** Sally hated Hugh for some reason; there was something about him which she did not like. **3** Five hundred pounds a year would not be enough for Peter and Daisy to survive on. **4** Clarissa was able to create a world around her, which was extraordinary. **5** Clarissa's relaxed and distant manner made Peter very frustrated. **6** Septimus was very keen to widen his knowledge. **7** He was one of the first men to join the Army. **8** Human nature said that such a bad person should die.

3 *(Suggested answer)*
THE WARREN SMITHS' MARRIAGE: lonely, unhappy/miserable, silent, insincere (Septimus)
THE DALLOWAYS: distant, lonely, loving, formal, social

4 Personal answers

5 **1** Rezia, when Septimus takes her hand and notices that she has taken off her wedding ring. **2** Sally Seton, arguing at Bourton with Hugh Whitbread. **3** Peter, telling himself that he is not in love with Clarissa any more, simply that he was thinking about her constantly after seeing her again. **4** Septimus, watching Rezia sitting at the table working on her hats. **5** Dr. Holmes, talking to Septimus. **6** Septimus, when Dr. Holmes comes into the room.

6 **1** T **2** T **3** F – Mrs. Hugh is a mouse-like little woman. Sally is wild, daring and romantic. **4** F – he is only two years older. **5** F – Peter *thinks* that he is no longer in love with her. **6** T **7** T **8** F – Septimus considers him *"a damned fool"*.

7 **1** Lucrezia Warren Smith **thought** that it was wicked. **2** She **informed** him that she had put the ring in her purse. **3** She **commented** that he thought of nothing but his own appearance. **4** She **was convinced** that it was the hat that mattered most. **5** Mr Brewer **insisted** that he had done his duty and that it was up to them.

8 Personal answers

9 **1** dismiss **2** proportion **3** weariness **4** deserted **5** sob **6** rug

10 Personal answers

Pages 74-77

1 **1** Sir William Bradshaw to Septimus, while making notes about him. **2** Septimus to Sir William, responding to his question about financial worries. **3** Rezia to Sir William, when he suggests a rest home for Septimus. **4** Septimus to Rezia, as they leave Sir William's. **5** Lady Bradshaw, talking about her husband during a dinner. **6** Rezia, talking about Sir William as she and Septimus walk down Harley Street.

2 *(Missing words in **bold**)* **1** When the Warren Smiths came into his room, Sir William Bradshaw saw that this was a case **of** extreme gravity. **2** Septimus felt that human nature had condemned him **to** death. **3** Sir William told Rezia that she would have to stay away **from** her husband. **4** Rezia felt that she and Septimus had been abandoned **by** Sir William. **5** Sir William had thirty years of experience **as** a doctor with a sense of proportion. **6** Fifteen years ago Lady Bradshaw had sacrificed her will **for** the sake **of** her husband's ambition.

3 **1** F – they have an appointment at 12 o'clock. **2** T **3** F – he has a deep prejudice against cultivated people. **4** T **5** T **6** F – fifteen years ago she would go salmon-fishing. **7** F – some patients call him insincere. **8** F – Rezia told Septimus that she did not like him.

4 **1** Sir William **inquired** whether Septimus had served with great distinction in the War. **2** Rezia **told** the doctor that he had been promoted. **3** Rezia **insisted** that Septimus had not meant to kill himself. **4** Sir William **informed** Septimus that they would teach him to rest. **5** Sir William **assured** Setpimus that he had a brilliant career before him.

5 **1** The income from Sir William Bradshaw's work, which would give him and Lady Bradshaw a financially comfortable life. **2** The number of patients and the considerable responsibility of his work made Sir William seem a very important person in company. **3** Sir William notes that Septimus repeated words and seemed to give them a special meaning. **4** Sir William is talking to Rezia and insisting that he never hurries his patients – an ironic observation, since he is doing exactly that with the Warren Smiths. **5** Lady Bradshaw had "gone under" 15 years ago – she had surrendered her will and her person to her husband, Sir William – but it had been so subtle that it was not possible to say exactly when and how. **6** The exciting fresh air of Harley Street, where Sir William practised, was not "available" to his patients, who went to stay in one of his special rest homes.

6 *(Suggested version in the Present, although can be in the Past)*
Septimus and Rezia **are** walking **down Harley Street** for a twelve o'clock appointment with Sir William Bradshaw. They see a **grey** motor-car outside his house. When Sir William first **sees** Septimus, he **realises** it is a serious case. Septimus tells him that he **has** been seeing Dr Holmes for **six weeks**. Sir William tells Rezia in **private** that Septimus **will need** plenty of rest in one of his homes in the **country**. She would **not** be able to visit him **during that time**. Septimus was very **un**happy at this suggestion and Sir William says that he will make all the arrangements. Rezia and Septimus leave and she **decides** that she **does not like** Sir William **at all**. It is **half** past one when they are in Oxford Street.

7a **1** magnificent – magnificence **2** unsuccessful – failure (*or* lack of success) **3** memorable – memorability **4** poor – poverty **5** contemplative – contemplation **6** silent – silence

7b **1** affection – affectionately **2** deception – deceptively **3** miracle – miraculously **4** happiness – happily **5** person – personally

7c Personal answers

8 Personal answers

Pages 88-91

1 **1** Richard **suggested** they sit down for five minutes. **2** Lady Bruton suddenly **asked** whether they knew who was in town. **3** He **confirmed** that Peter Walsh had come back. **4** Lady Bruton **insisted** that they would hear the story from Peter himself. **5** Clarissa **told** Elizabeth that Kilman had arrived just as they had finished lunch.

2 **1** Although Hugh always brought flowers, Lady Bruton preferred Richard Dalloway. **2** Hugh was afraid (**that**) he would not be able to find a permanent job for Peter because **of** a flaw in his character. **3** After Hugh had finished **the** letter **to** the *Times*, Lady Bruton was enthusiastic and called **it** a masterpiece. **4** Richard wanted to give Clarissa **a** bunch **of** flowers and tell her that he loved **her**.

3 Personal answers

4 **1** had been doing badly **2** produced **3** was very fond of **4** dressed to match **5** reflected **6** as if he were about to...

5 **1** Lady Bruton to Hugh Whitbread and Richard Dalloway **2** Hugh Whitbread (at lunch) **3** Richard Dalloway to Lady Bruton **4** Clarissa (after reading Mrs. Marsham's note) **5** Richard to Clarissa **6** Clarissa to Richard

6 **1** F **2** T **3** T **4** – she knows it already **5** F – they just don't know how to say good-bye **6** T **7** T

7 **1** clearly **2** imperfect **3** exuberant **4** frustratedly **5** untrained **6** seemingly

8 (*Synonyms in **bold***) **1** She was quite **unconscious** that she was being **watched**. **2** She **could not bear** to see them together. **3** People who **shared** her views... **4** She **could not afford** to buy pretty clothes. **5** She had almost **burst into tears**... **6** She had **had to go**.

Pages 102-105

1 **1** At her age, Miss Kilman did not dress to please people. **2** When Clarissa saw the old lady opposite, she wanted to cry. **3** Miss Kilman felt that Mrs Dalloway had wasted her life. **4** Elizabeth much preferred to be left alone in the country.

2 **1** Miss Kilman (about Mrs Dalloway) **2** Mrs Dalloway to Miss Kilman **3** Miss Kilman to Elizabeth **4** Clarissa to Elizabeth **5** Elizabeth (sitting on the bus) **6** Miss Kilman to Elizabeth

3 **1** Miss Kilman **thought** that Clarissa Dalloway was a fool and had wasted her life. **2** Clarissa (leant over the banisters and) **reminded** Elizabeth about the party. **3** Miss Kilman **insisted** that she never went to parties. **4** Doris Kilman **asked** Elizabeth not to forget her altogether. **5** Miss Kilman **told** Elizabeth that she had not quite finished yet.

4a **1** converse **2** suffer **3** please **4** see **5** breathe

4b **1** traditional **2** interesting **3** sorrowful **4** comfortable **5** religious

5 **1** F – Miss Kilman is younger. **2** F – her family comes from Germany. **3** T **4** T **5** F **6** T **7** F – they held public service without being brilliant.

6a (*Suggestions*)
sinister, strange, extraordinary, shocked, touching, terrible, determined, difficult, alone, charming, beautiful, serene, bored, odd, busy, lazy

6b Personal answers

7 Personal answers

8 **1** the Strand **2** fair **3** distant **4** burst into the room **5** collided with **6** considered **7** putting **8** moved off

Pages 116-119

1 **1** T **2** T **3** F – Septimus wanted her to read Shakespeare (in English). **4** T **5** F – he hears the ambulance but doesn't know what has happened. **6** F – it is in a blue envelope. **7** T **8** T

2a **1** inconvenient **2** efficient **3** regrettable **4** theoretical **5** enviable

2b **1** melancholy **2** bravery **3** certainty **4** upset **5** contentedness

3 Personal answers

4 **1** Septimus looked proudly at Rezia, who turned the hat on the tips of her fingers. **2** When people stopped to let the ambulance pass, Peter was impressed. **3** If Peter had married Clarissa, it would not have been a success. **4** Peter decided to go to Clarissa's party so that he could ask Richard Dalloway about the situation in India.

5 **1** b **2** f **3** e **4** d **5** c **6** a

6a **1** ordinary **2** inconceivable **3** subtle **4** bald **5** off

6b Personal answers

6c **1** dug **2** took off **3** hesitated **4** rushing out **5** gave up

6d Personal answers

7 **1** Septimus **noticed** that the hat was too small for Mrs. Peters. **2** He **wondered** what right Bradshaw had to say 'must' to him. **3** Holmes **assured** her that he had come as a friend. **4** She **decided** that she would not allow him to see her husband. **5** Dr. Holmes **insisted** that they should let her sleep.

8 **1** Clarissa (at the party) **2** Sally to Clarissa **3** Mrs. Hilbery to Clarissa **4** Mrs. Bradshaw to Clarissa **5** Peter to Sally **6** Richard Dalloway to his daughter

Pages 130-131

1a **1** enjoyment **2** laughter **3** murmur **4** criticism **5** dislike **6** anticipation

1b **1** intimacy **2** devotion **3** precision **4** charm

2 **1** T **2** T **3** F – everybody pretends not to be interested. **4** F – she is crying because she is thinking about her mother. **5** T **6** T **7** F – he plays with his pocket-knife when he is excited. **8** T

3 **1** She **remarked** how awfully good it was of them to come. **2** Clarissa **replied** that she couldn't believe it. **3** She **was convinced** that Richard had enjoyed his lunch party. **4** She **decided** she couldn't stay. **5** Peter **wondered** where Clarissa was.

4a **1** annoying **2** critical **3** pleasing **4** different **5** supernatural **6** delirious
4b Personal answers

Page 140
Personal answers

Read for Pleasure: *Mrs Dalloway* 戴洛維夫人

作　　者：Virginia Woolf

改　　寫：Richard Larkham

繪　　畫：Antonio Marinoni

照　　片：ELI Archive

責任編輯：傅　薇

封面設計：涂　慧

出　　版：商務印書館（香港）有限公司

　　　　　香港筲箕灣耀興道 3 號東滙廣場 8 樓

　　　　　http://www.commercialpress.com.hk

發　　行：香港聯合書刊物流有限公司

　　　　　香港新界大埔汀麗路 36 號中華商務印刷大廈 3 字樓

印　　刷：中華商務彩色印刷有限公司

　　　　　香港新界大埔汀麗路 36 號中華商務印刷大廈 14 字樓

版　　次：2016 年 11 月第 1 版第 1 次印刷

　　　　　© 2016 商務印書館（香港）有限公司

　　　　　ISBN 978 962 07 0484 0

　　　　　Printed in Hong Kong

　　　　　版權所有　不得翻印